PENGUIN BOOKS

THE SNAPPER

Roddy Doyle is the author of six novels. The first three—
The Commitments, The Snapper, and 1991 Booker Prize nomi-
nee *The Van*—are available both singly and in one volume
as *The Barrytown Trilogy,* published by Penguin. In 1993
Paddy Clarke Ha Ha Ha won the Booker Prize and became
an international bestseller. Doyle's next novel was the ac-
claimed *The Woman Who Walked Into Doors* which was also a
bestseller and was followed by *A Star Called Henry.* Doyle
has also written for the stage and the screen: the plays
Brownbread and *War;* the film adaptations of *The Commitments* (as co-writer), *The Snapper,* and *The Van; Stolen
Nights* (an original screenplay); the four-part television
series *Family* for the BBC; and the television play *Hell for
Leather.* Roddy Doyle is also the author of the children's
book *The Giggler Treatment.* He lives in Dublin.

THE SNAPPER
RODDY DOYLE

PENGUIN BOOKS

PENGUIN BOOKS
Published by the Penguin Group
Penguin Books USA Inc.,
375 Hudson Street, New York, New York 10014, U.S.A.
Penguin Books Ltd, 27 Wrights Lane,
London W8 5TZ, England
Penguin Books Australia Ltd, Ringwood,
Victoria, Australia
Penguin Books Canada Ltd, 10 Alcorn Avenue,
Toronto, Ontario, Canada M4V 3B2
Penguin Books (N.Z.) Ltd, 182–190 Wairau Road,
Auckland 10, New Zealand

Penguin Books Ltd, Registered Offices:
Harmondsworth, Middlesex, England

First published in Great Britain by
Martin Secker & Warburg Limited 1990
Published in Penguin Books 1992

17 19 20 18 16

PUBLISHER'S NOTE
This is a work of fiction. Names, characters, places, and incidents either
are the product of the author's imagination or are used fictitiously, and
any resemblance to actual persons, living or dead, events, or locales is
entirely coincidental.

LIBRARY OF CONGRESS CATALOGING IN PUBLICATION DATA
Doyle, Roddy. 1958–
The snapper/Roddy Doyle.
p. cm.
ISBN 0 14 01.7167 3
I. Title.
PR6054.O95S64   1992
823'.914 — dc20   91–43433

Printed in the United States of America
Set in 11 pt. Sabon

This book is dedicated to

Belinda

—You're wha'? said Jimmy Rabbitte Sr.

He said it loudly.

—You heard me, said Sharon.

Jimmy Jr was upstairs in the boys' room doing his D.J. practice. Darren was in the front room watching Police Academy II on the video. Les was out. Tracy and Linda, the twins, were in the front room annoying Darren. Veronica, Mrs Rabbitte, was sitting opposite Jimmy Sr at the kitchen table.

Sharon was pregnant and she'd just told her father that she thought she was. She'd told her mother earlier, before the dinner.

—Oh —my Jaysis, said Jimmy Sr.

He looked at Veronica. She looked tired. He looked at Sharon again.

—That's shockin', he said.

Sharon said nothing.

—Are yeh sure? said Jimmy Sr.

—Yeah. Sort of.

—Wha'?

—Yeah.

Jimmy Sr wasn't angry. He probably wouldn't be either, but it all seemed very unfair.

—You're only nineteen, he said.

—I'm twenty.

—You're only twenty.

—I know what age I am, Daddy.

—Now, there's no need to be gettin' snotty, said Jimmy Sr.

—Sorry, said Sharon.

She nearly meant it.

—I'm the one tha' should be gettin' snotty, said Jimmy Sr.

Sharon made herself smile. She was happy with the way things were going so far.

—It's shockin', said Jimmy Sr again, —so it is. Wha' do you think o' this?

He was talking to Veronica.

—I don't know, said Veronica.

—Is tha' the best yeh can do, Veronica?

—Well, what do YOU think?

Jimmy Sr creased his face and held it that way for a second.

—I don't know, he said. —I should give ou', I suppose. An' throw a wobbler or somethin'. But ——what's the point?

Veronica nodded. She looked very tired now.

Jimmy Sr continued.

—If she was —

He turned to Sharon.

—You should've come to us earlier —before, yeh know —an' said you were goin' to get pregnant.

The three of them tried to laugh.

—Then we could've done somethin' abou' it. ——My God, though.

No one said anything. Then Jimmy Sr spoke to Sharon again.

—You're absolutely sure now? Positive?

—Yeah, I am. I done —

—Did, said Veronica.

—I did the test.

—The test? said Jimmy Sr. —Oh. —Did yeh go in by yourself?

—Yeah, said Sharon.

—Did yeh? Fair play to yeh, said Jimmy Sr. —I'd never've thought o' tha'.

Sharon and Veronica looked at each other, and grinned quickly.

Jimmy Sr got down to business.

—Who was it?

—Wha'? ——Oh. I don't know.

—Ah now, Jaysis —!

—No, I do know.

—Well, then?

—I'm not tellin'.

Jimmy Sr could feel himself getting a bit angry now. That was better.

—Now, look —

They heard Jimmy Jr from up in the boys' room.

—THIS IS JIMMY RABBITTE – ALL – OVER – IRELAND.

—Will yeh listen to tha' fuckin' eejit, said his father.

—Leave him alone, said Veronica.

Jimmy Sr stared at the ceiling.

—I don't know.

Then he turned to Sharon again.

—Why won't yeh tell us?

Sharon said nothing. Jimmy Sr saw her eyes filling with water.

—Don't start tha', he told her. —Just tell us.

—I can't, Sharon told the table.

—Why not?

——I just can't, righ'.

Jimmy Sr looked across at Veronica and shook his head. He'd never been able to cope with answers like that. If Sharon had been one of the boys he'd have walloped her.

Veronica looked worried now. She wasn't sure she really wanted to know the answer.

—Is he married? Jimmy Sr asked.

—Oh my God, said Veronica.

—No, he's not! said Sharon.

—Well, that's somethin', I suppose, said Jimmy Sr.
—Then why —

Veronica started crying.

—Ah Veronica, stop tha'.

Linda ran in.

—Daddy, Darren's after hittin' me.

She was getting ready to cry.

—Jesus! Another one, said Jimmy Sr.

Then he spoke to Linda.

—I'll go in in a minute an' I'll hit Darren an' you can watch me hittin' him.

—Can I?

—Yeah, yeh can. Now get ou' or I'll practise on you first.

Linda squealed and ran away from him. She stopped at the safe side of the kitchen door.

—Can Tracy watch as well? she asked.

—She can o' course. Now, your mammy an' Sharon an' me are havin' a chat, so leave us alone.

Jimmy Sr looked at the two women. The crying had stopped.

—THIS IS JIMMY RABBITTE — ALL — OVER — IRELAND.

—Oh good Jesus, what a house! ——Is he queer or wha' is he? Jimmy Sr asked Sharon.

—No, he's not. He's alrigh'; leave him alone.

—I don't know, said Jimmy Sr. —Tha' gear he wears. He had his trous —

—That's only the fashion.

—I suppose so. But, Jaysis.

He looked at Veronica. She just looked tired again.

—This is an awful shock, Sharon, he said. —Isn't it, Veronica?

—Definitely.

—Make us a cup o' tea there, love, will yeh.

—Make it yourself, said Veronica.

—I'll make it, said Sharon.

—Good girl, said Jimmy Sr. —Mind yourself against the table there. Good girl. ——You're sure now he's not married?

—Yeah, he's not, said Sharon, at the sink.

—Then why won't yeh tell us then?

—Look, said Sharon.

She turned to face him.

—I can't, an' I'm not goin' to.

She turned back to plug in the kettle.

—Will he marry you? Jimmy Sr asked her.

—No. I don't think so.

—The louser. That's cheatin', tha' is.

—It's not a game! said Veronica.

—I know, I know tha', Veronica. But it's his fault as much as Sharon's. Whoever he is. ——It was his flute tha'—

—Daddy!

—Well, it was.

—It's no wonder they all talk the way they do, Veronica gave out to Jimmy Sr.

—Ah, lay off, Veronica, will yeh.

They heard a scream from the front room.

—Hang on till I sort this young fella ou', said Jimmy Sr.

He marched out of the kitchen.

—He's taking it well, said Veronica.

—Yeah, said Sharon. —So are you.

—Ah sure —

—I was afraid you'd throw me ou'.

—I never thought of that, mind you. ——It's not right though, said Veronica.

She looked straight at Sharon.

—I suppose it's not, said Sharon.

Jimmy Sr came back, rubbing his hands and calling Darren a sneaky little bastard. He sat down and saw the tea waiting for him.

—Aah, lovely.

He sipped.

—Fuck! ——Sorry, Veronica; excuse me. It's very hot.

—He's started saying Excuse me. After twenty-two years.

—Good luck, Jimmy Jr roared from the front door, and then he slammed it.

—He shuts the door like a normal man annyway. That's somethin', I suppose.

—He's alrigh', said Sharon.

Jimmy Sr now said something he'd heard a good few times on the telly.

—D'yeh want to keep it?

—Wha' d'yeh mean?

—D'yeh —d'you want to keep it, like?

—He wants to know if you want to have an abortion, said Veronica. —The eejit.

—I do not! said Jimmy Sr.

This was true. He was sorry now he'd said it.

—There's no way I'd have an abortion, said Sharon.

—Good. You're right.

—Abortion's murder.

—It is o' course.

Then he thought of something and he had to squirt his tea back into the cup. He could hear his heart. And feel it.

He looked at Sharon.

—He isn't a black, is he?

—No!

6

He believed her. The three of them started laughing.

—One o' them students, yeh know, Jimmy Sr explained.
—With a clatter o' wives back in Africa.

—Stop that.

Jimmy Sr's tea was finished.

—That was grand, Sharon, thanks, he said. —An' you're def'ny not goin' to tell us who it is?

—No. ——Sorry.

—Never mind the Sorry. ——I think you should tell us. I'm not goin' to kill him or annythin'.

Sharon said nothing.

Jimmy Sr pushed his chair back from the table.

—There's no point in anny more talkin' then, I suppose. Your mind's obviously made up, Sharon.

He stood up.

—A man needs a pint after all tha', he said.

—Is that all? said Veronica, shocked.

—Wha' d'yeh mean, Veronica?

—It's a terrible —Veronica started.

But she couldn't really go on. She thought that Sharon's news deserved a lot more attention, and some sort of punishment. As far as Veronica was concerned this was the worst thing that had ever happened the family. But she couldn't really explain why, not really. And she knew that, anyway, nothing could be done about it. Maybe it wouldn't be so bad once she got used to it.

Then she thought of something.

—The neighbours, she said.

—Wha' abou' them? said Jimmy Sr.

Veronica thought for a bit.

—What'll they say? she then said.

—You don't care wha' tha' lot says, do yeh? said Jimmy Sr.

——Yes. I do.

—Ah now, Veronica.

He sat down.

Sharon spoke.

—They'll have a laugh when they find ou' an' they'll try an' guess who I'm havin' it for. An' that's all. ——An' anyway, I don't care.

—An' that's the important thing, Jimmy Sr told Veronica.

Veronica didn't look convinced.

—Sure look, said Jimmy Sr. —The O'Neill young ones have had kids, the both o' them. An' —an' the Bells would be the same 'cept they don't have anny daughters, but yeh know wha' I mean.

—Dawn O'Neill had her baby for Paddy Bell, Sharon reminded him.

—She did o' course, said Jimmy Sr.

He stood up.

—So there now, Veronica, he said. —Fuck the neighbours.

Veronica tried to look as if she'd been won over. She wanted to go up to bed. She nodded.

Jimmy Sr had a nice idea.

—Are yeh comin' for a drink, Sharon?

—No thanks, Daddy. I'll stay in tonigh'.

—Ah, go on.

—Alrigh', Sharon smiled.

—Good girl. Yeh may as well ——Veronica?

—'M? ——Ah no, no thanks.

—Go on.

—No. I'm goin' up to bed.

—I'd go up with yeh only I've a throat on me.

Veronica smiled.

—You're sure now? said Jimmy Sr.

—Yep, said Veronica.

Sharon went for her jacket.

—Will I bring yeh home a few chips? Jimmy Sr asked Veronica.

—I'll be asleep.

—Fair enough.

Jimmy Sr stopped at the front door and roared back to Veronica.

—Cheerio now, Granny.

Then he laughed, and slammed the door harder than Jimmy Jr had.

* * *

Jimmy Sr came back with the drinks and sat in beside Sharon. He hated the tables up here, in the lounge. You couldn't get your legs in under them. Sharon couldn't either. She sat side-saddle.

—Thanks a lot, Daddy, said Sharon when she'd poured the Coke in with the vodka.

—Ah, no problem, said Jimmy Sr.

He'd never had a drink with Sharon before. He watched his pint settling, something he never did when he was downstairs in the bar. He only came up here on Sundays, and now.

He turned to Sharon and spoke softly.

—When's it due an' annyway?

—November.

Jimmy Sr did a few quick sums in his head.

—You're three months gone.

—No. Nearly.

—Yeh should've told us earlier.

—I know. ——I was scared to.

—Ah, Sharon. ——I still think you should tell us who the da is.

—You can think away then.

Jimmy Sr couldn't help grinning. She'd always been like that.

—I thought your mammy took it very well, he said.

—Yeah, Sharon agreed. —She was great.

—Cos she's a bit ol' fashioned like tha'. Set in her ways.

—Yeah. No, she was great. So were you.

—Ah, now.

They said nothing after that for a bit. Jimmy Sr could think of nothing else to say. He looked around him: kids and yuppies. He sat there, feeling far from home. The lads would all be downstairs by now. Jimmy Sr had a good one he'd heard in work for them, about a harelip in a sperm-bank. He loved Sharon but, if the last five minutes were anything to go by, she was shocking drinking company.

He noticed Jimmy Jr up at the stools with his pals.

—There's Jimmy, he said.

—Yeah, said Sharon.

—That's an awful lookin' shower he hangs around with.

—They're alrigh'.

—The haircuts on them, look.

—That's only the fashion these days. Leave them alone.

—I s'pose so, said Jimmy Sr.

And they stopped again.

There was only an hour to closing time but Jimmy Sr wasn't sure he'd be able to stick it.

—Wha' does Jimmy be doin' up there when he's shoutin', yeh know, abou' bein' all over Ireland? he asked Sharon.

—He wants to be a D.J.

—A wha'?

—A D.J. A disc jockey.

—Wha'; like Larry Gogan?

—Yeah. Sort of.

—Jaysis, said Jimmy Sr.

He'd had enough.

He'd spotted a gang of Sharon's friends over past Jimmy Jr and his pals.

—There's those friends o' yours, Sharon, he said.

Sharon knew what he was at.

—Oh yeah, she said.

—D'yeh want to go over to them?

—I don't mind.

—They'd be better company than your oul' fella annyway, wha'.

—Ah no.

—Go on. Yeh may as well go over. I don't mind.

—I can't leave you on your own.

—Ah sure, said Jimmy Sr. —I can go down an' see if
there's annyone downstairs.

Sharon grinned. So did Jimmy Sr. He still felt guilty
though, so he got a fiver out and handed it to Sharon.

—Ah, there's no need, Daddy.

—There is o' course, said Jimmy Sr.

He moved in closer to her.

—It's not every day yeh find ou' you're goin' to be a
granda.

He'd just thought of that now and he had to stop himself
from letting his eyes water. He often did things like that,
gave away pounds and fivers or said nice things; little things
that made him like himself.

He patted Sharon's shoulder. He was standing up, but he
stopped.

—Hang on a sec, he said. —I'll wait till your man passes.

Sharon looked.

—Who?

—Burgess there, the bollix. Excuse me, Sharon. I can't
stand him.

—I've seen yeh talkin' to him loads o' times.

—He traps me. An' Darren's his goalie this year. He'd
drop him if I got snotty with him.

—Oh. Yeah.

—It's alrigh' now, said Jimmy Sr, and he stood up again.
—The coast's clear. See yeh later.

Jimmy Sr trotted out, and down to the lads in the bar.

Sharon took her vodka and her jacket and her bag and went across to Jackie O'Keefe, Mary Curran and Yvonne Burgess, her friends; the gang.

—Hiyis, she said when she got there.

—Oh, howyeh, Sharon.

—Hiyeh, Sharon.

—Howyeh, Sharon.

—Hiyis, said Sharon.

—Put your bag over here, Sharon, look, said Yvonne.

—Thanks, said Sharon. —Hiyeh, Jackie. Haven't seen yeh in ages.

—She's been busy, said Mary.

Yvonne sniggered.

—How's Greg? Sharon asked Jackie.

Yvonne sniggered again.

—Fuck off, you, said Jackie. —He's grand, Sharon.

—They're goin' on their holliers together, Mary told Sharon.

—Dirty bitch, said Yvonne.

They laughed.

—Fuck off, will yeh, said Jackie. —We're not goin' for definite.

She explained.

—He mightn't be able to take the time off.

—Yeh see, Sharon, said Yvonne. —You've got to understand, Greg's a very important person.

—Fuck off, Burgess, said Jackie, but she was grinning.

—Where're yeh goin'? Sharon asked Jackie.

—Rimini. In Italy.

—Lovely.

—Yeah.

—Yeh can go for a swim with the Pope, said Yvonne.

They laughed.

—Cos there'll be fuck all else to do there, Yvonne finished.

—She's just jealous, said Mary.

—Of wha'? said Yvonne ———

Mary changed the subject.

—Anny news, Sharon? she asked.

—No, said Sharon. —Not really.

*   *   *

Sharon told no one else yet.

She bought a book in Easons and read about the first fourteen weeks of pregnancy and waited for the changes to happen; the breasts swelling, the urinating, the nausea and that. She looked at herself in her parents' wardrobe mirror. She looked the same. And from the side; the same as well. She was ten weeks and two days pregnant. She didn't bother including the hours and minutes, but she nearly could have. The book said that the real changes started after the tenth week. And that was now.

Her nipples were going to get darker. She didn't mind that too much. The veins in her breasts would become more prominent. Sharon didn't like the sound of that. That worried her. She wondered would they be horrible and knobbly like her Auntie Mona's varicose veins. The joints between her pelvic bones would be widening. She hoped they wouldn't pinch a sciatic nerve, which ran from her arse down through the back of her legs, because she had to stand a lot of the time in work and a pinched sciatic nerve would be a killer. She read about her hormones and what they were doing to her. She could picture them; little roundy balls with arms and legs. She hoped her bowel movements stayed fairly regular. Her uterus would soon be pressing into her bladder. What worried her most was the bit about vaginal secretions. They'd make her itchy, it said. That would be really terrible in work, fuckin' murder. Or when she was out. She'd have preferred a pinched sciatic nerve.

She hoped these changes came one at a time.

She read about eating. Nearly everything she normally ate was wrong. She decided she'd follow the instructions in the book. She wasn't getting sick in the mornings but she started having dry toast for her breakfast, just to be on the safe side. It was good for morning sickness. She ate raw carrots. She took celery home from work and chewed that. Jimmy Sr banned the carrots and the celery when the telly was on, except during the ads. If she didn't go easy on the carrots, he said, she'd give birth to a fuckin' rabbit. And there were enough bunnies in the house already.

She ploughed through her book, about three pages a night. It was hard going, and frightening. There was a lot more to being pregnant than she'd thought. And there was so much that could go wrong.

She didn't feel pregnant yet, not really.

She read about the feelings she might have at this stage. She might, she read, feel increased sensuality. She looked that up in Darren's dictionary and that wasn't how she felt at all. She might feel like she was in love: no way. She might feel great excitement: ——no.

She was sitting between Jimmy Sr and Veronica a few days after she'd told them the news. Blankety Blank was over. The panel were waving out at them. Jimmy Sr stuck his fingers up at them. Darren laughed.

—Your man, Rolf Harris, is an awful gobshite, said Jimmy Sr. —I've always said it.

—He's a great painter, said Veronica.

—He is in his hole a great painter, said Jimmy Sr. —He slaps a bit o' paint around an' if it looks like somethin' he says it an' if it doesn't he starts singin' Two Little Boys Had Two Little Toys. To distract us.

—He's good for the kids, said Veronica.

—He's good for the bowels, said Jimmy Sr. —You don't like him, do yeh, Darren?

—No way.

—I don't like him either, said Tracy.

—I don't like him either, said Linda.

—There now, Veronica, said Jimmy Sr.

—What's perception? Sharon asked.

—Wha?

—What's perception?

—Sweat, Jimmy Sr told her. —Why?

Sharon whispered to Jimmy Sr.

—It says my perception might be heightened when I'm pregnant.

—Yeh smell alrigh' from here, love, said Jimmy Sr.

He leaned over.

—What's the buke abou'?

—Pregnancy.

—Jaysis, d'yeh need a buke to be pregnant these days?

—I didn't have a book, said Veronica.

—Shhh! went Jimmy Sr.

—You wouldn't've been able to read it, Ma, said Darren.

The remote control hit his shoulder and bounced off his head.

—Wha' was tha' for!? he cried.

His hand tried to cover both sore spots.

—Mind your own business, you, said Jimmy Sr. —Don't look at me like tha', son, or I'll ——Say you're sorry to your mother.

—I was on'y —

—SAY YOU'RE SORRY.

——————Sorry.

—PROPERLY.

—I'm sorry, Ma.

—You don't look it, said Veronica.

—I can't help it.

—You get that from your father.

—It's not all he'll get from his father, said Jimmy Sr.

—Turn on Sky there, he barked at Darren, —for the wrestlin'.

—His master's voice, said Veronica.

—No chips for you tonigh', Jimmy Sr told her.

—Aw.

Jimmy Sr pointed at a diagram in Sharon's book.

—What's tha' supposed to be? he asked her.

—The inside of a woman, said Sharon, softly.

—Jaysis, said Jimmy Sr. —Sky, I said. That's RTE 2. Look at the wavy lines, look. That's RTE 2. It's one o' their farmin' programmes.

Linda and Tracy giggled.

Jimmy Sr studied the diagram.

—Where's it all fit? he wanted to know. —Is this an Irish buke, Sharon?

—No. English.

—Ah, said Jimmy Sr.

—Is Sharon havin' a baby? Linda asked.

—No! said Jimmy Sr.

—Are yeh, Sharon?

—Are yeh havin' a baby, Sharon? said Tracy.

—NO, I SAID.

—Sharon, are yeh?

—Aaah! said Jimmy Sr.

—No, I'm not, Sharon told them. —A friend o' mine is, that's all.

—Ah, said Tracy, very disappointed.

—Ma? said Linda.

—Mammy, said Veronica.

—Mammy. Will you be havin' more babies?

—Oh my Jaysis, said Jimmy Sr. —Here. Here. Come here.

He dug into his pockets. He'd no change, so he gave Linda a pound note.

—Go ou' an' buy sweets. ——Say Thank —

16

But they were gone. Jimmy Sr saw Darren looking at him.

—What're you lookin' at? ——Here.

It was a pound.

—Thanks, Da. Rapid.

—Get ou'. ——I think yeh'd better read tha' buke up in your room, Sharon. I can't afford to do tha' every nigh'.

—D'yeh think they know? Sharon asked him.

—Not at all, said Jimmy Sr. —They'll have forgotten all abou' it once they have their faces stuffed with —with Trigger Bars an' Cadbury's fuckin' Cream Eggs.

—Stop that.

—Sorry, Veronica. ——Annyway sure, we'll have to tell them some time annyway, won't we?

—Yeah. I suppose so. ——Yeah. I hadn't thought o' tha', said Sharon.

—I have, Veronica told her.

Sharon brought the book upstairs.

She read on. She might feel shock: no, not now. She might feel a loss of individuality. She might feel she didn't matter: no. Like a vessel: no. Loveless: yeah ——not really. Scared: a bit. Sick: not yet. Not ready for pregnancy: sort of, but not really.

What she really felt, she decided later in bed, was confused. There was so much. And she wouldn't have really known that if she hadn't bought the bleedin' book.

But she wanted to know. She wanted to know exactly what was going to happen, what was happening even now. She put her hand on her stomach: nothing.

*   *   *

She felt a bit impatient too. Sometimes she didn't think anything was going to happen. She hoped the changes came soon. She was ready for it; getting bigger, backache, and the rest of it. In a way she wanted it. She didn't mind people knowing she was pregnant —as long as no one knew who'd helped her —but she couldn't go around telling everyone. She could never have done that. Once she started getting bigger, then they'd know. Then they could laugh and talk about it and try and guess who she'd done it with, and then leave her alone.

Though she'd have to tell her friends, Jackie and them.

* * *

Jimmy Sr woke up. His neck was killing him. He hated falling asleep sitting on the couch, but he'd had a few pints with the lads after the pitch and putt, so he didn't know he was falling asleep till now, after he'd woken up. He tried to stretch, and lift his head up.

—Ah —! ——fuck——

He shook himself. His chin was wet, and a bit of his shirt.

—Ah Jaysis, he gave out to himself. —Yeh fuckin' baby, yeh.

He looked at the telly. Cricket.

—Ah, fuckin' hell.

He always got angry the minute he saw cricket. It really annoyed him, everything about it; the umpires, the white gear, the commentators, the whole fuckin' lot.

He couldn't find the remote control, so he had to stand up. When he got to the telly he didn't bother looking to see if there was anything else on. He just turned it off.

His mouth and throat were dry. He needed Coke, or anything fizzy and cold.

Veronica was in the kitchen, at the table, cutting material.

—Is it still Saturday? said Jimmy Sr.

—The dead arose, said Veronica.

Jimmy Sr went to the fridge. He bent down and took out a large yellow-pack bottle, empty.

—Fuck it annyway!

—Now now.

—There was loads in it this mornin'. I only had a few slugs.

—Jimmy had the rest of it before he went to work, Veronica told him. —He didn't look very well.

—Fuck'm, said Jimmy Sr. —Why can't he buy his own?

—Why can't YOU buy your own?

—I bought this one!

—Excuse ME. I bought it.

—With my fuckin' money.

Veronica said nothing. Jimmy Sr sat down. He shouldn't have shouted at her. He felt guilty now. He'd send one of the kids to get her a choc-ice when one of them came in.

—What's tha' you're makin', Veronica? he asked.

Veronica glanced at him over her glasses.

—A skirt. For Linda, she said.

—No one'll run her over in the dark annyway, wha', said Jimmy Sr.

The material was very bright, shiny red.

—Ha ha, said Veronica. —It's for their majorettes.

—Their wha'?

—Majorettes. You know. Marching to music.

—Wha'? Like in American football?

—That's right.

This worried Jimmy Sr.

—They're a bit young for tha', aren't they?

—Don't be stupid, said Veronica. —They're doing it in school.

—Oh, fair enough so, said Jimmy Sr. —What's for the dinner?

—You had your dinner, Veronica reminded him.

She put the scissors down on the table. That was that for one day. Her eyes were sore.

—For the tea, said Jimmy Sr.

————A fry, said Veronica.

—Lovely, said Jimmy Sr. —An' some fried bread maybe?

Veronica looked across. There was one full sliced pan and most of another one.

—Right, she said. —Okay.

—Veronica, said Jimmy Sr. —I love yeh.

—Umf, said Veronica.

The back door opened and Les charged through the kitchen. They heard him walloping the stairs as he ran up to the boys' room.

—Don't say hello or ann'thin'! Jimmy Sr roared.

There wasn't an answer. The door slammed.

—No one just closes doors annymore, said Jimmy Sr. —Did yeh ever notice tha', Veronica?

Veronica had her head in the fridge. She was wiping some dried milk off the inside of the door.

—They either slam them or they leave the fuckin' things open, said Jimmy Sr. —I went into the jacks there this mornin' an' Linda was sittin' in there readin' a comic. Or it might've been Tracy.

—You should have knocked, said Veronica.

—The door was open, said Jimmy Sr. —An open jacks door means the jacks is empty. Everywhere in the world except in this house. Walk into the jacks in this house an' you'll find a twin, or Jimmy pukin', or Leslie wankin' —

—Stop that!

—Sorry. ————That's the sort o' stuff they should be teachin' them in school. Not Irish or —or German. Shuttin' jacks doors an' sayin' Hello an' tha' sort o' thing. Manners.

—Will you look who's talking about manners, said Veronica, and she stabbed a sausage a couple of times and turned it, and stabbed it again.

Jimmy Jr came in, from work.

—Howyis, he said.

—Get stuffed, you, said Jimmy Sr.

—Manners! said Veronica.

—Listen here, you, said Jimmy Sr. —You're not to be drinkin' all the Coke in the mornin', righ'. Buy your own.

—I put me money into the house, said Jimmy Jr.

—Is tha' wha' yeh call it? Yeh couldn't wipe your arse with the amount you give your mother.

He pointed at the sausages.

—D'you know how much they cost, do yeh?

—Do YOU know? Veronica asked him.

Darren came in the back door, and saved Jimmy Sr.

—Did yeh win, Darren? he asked.

—Yeah, said Darren. —I saved a penno.

—Did yeh? Ah, good man. Good man yourself. Wha' score?

—Two-one.

—Yeh let one in.

—It wasn't my fault.

—Course it wasn't.

—Muggah McCarthy let it through his legs an' —

Veronica looked at Darren.

—Get up, you, and wash some of that muck off you.

The twins came in as Darren went out.

—Ma, Da, said Linda. —Can we keep this?

It was a pup, a tiny black wad of fluff with four skinny legs and a tail that would have looked long on a fully grown dog. It was shaking in Linda's hands, terrified.

—No, said Veronica, and —Yeah, said Jimmy Sr at the same time. —Yeh can o' course.

—Not after the last one, said Veronica. —They never stopped crying after Bonzo got run over. And Darren and Sharon.

—And you, said Jimmy Sr.

—Ah, Mammy. We won't cry this time. Sure we won't, Tracy?

—Yeah, said Tracy. —We'll tie the gate so he can't get ou'.

—No, I said.

—Ah, Ma-mmy! Let's.

—Who'll feed it? Veronica wanted to know.

—Wha' is it? said Jimmy Sr.

—A dog, said Linda. —It'll grow bigger.

—Will it? said Jimmy Sr. —That's very clever.

Veronica laughed. She couldn't help it.

Tracy pounced.

—Can we keep it, Mammy? Can we?

——Alright, said Veronica.

Jimmy Sr beamed at her.

—When was the last time you brushed your teeth? she asked him.

—This mornin'!

—With Guinness, was it?

She looked at the twins.

—You're to feed it, the two of you. ——An' it's not to come into the house.

—The 'Malley's dog had it, Linda told them. —He had loads o' them.

—Can we get another one, Ma? One each.

—No!

—Aah.

—No.

—One'll do yis, said Jimmy Sr. —Show us it here.

Linda handed the pup to Jimmy Sr.

Jimmy Jr walked back in.

—What's tha'? A rat?

—It is not a rat, Jimmy Rabbitte, said Tracy. —It's a dog.

—It's a dog, righ', said Linda.

It was warm and quivering. Jimmy Sr could feel its bones.

—Wha' sort of a dog is it but? he asked.

—Black, said Tracy.

—Go 'way! said Jimmy Jr.

—I'm your new da, Jimmy Sr told it.

They all laughed.

—An', look it. There's your mammy makin' the tea.

He made its paw wave at Veronica. Linda and Tracy were delighted. They couldn't wait to do that.

—Give us it, said Linda, and she pulled at it.

—Easy! ——for Jaysis sake, said Jimmy Sr. —You'll break the poor little bastard.

He lifted it up by the skin at the back of its neck and looked under it.

—It's a young fella, he told Veronica.

—Thank God, said Veronica.

—How do yeh know tha'? Tracy wanted to know.

—It's written there. Look.

—It isn't. ——Where is it?

Then the pup puked on Jimmy Sr's shoulder.

—Oh, look it, said Linda.

She tried to rub it off before her mammy saw it and changed her mind.

—Leave it, leave it, said Jimmy Sr. —What're you laughin' at?

—Nothin' much, said Jimmy Jr.

—Put it in the back, said Veronica.

Jimmy Sr put the pup on the table so he could get to the sink and clean his shoulder. It stood there, rattling, its paws slipping on the formica, and pissed on it.

Tracy grabbed it and ran for the door and Jimmy Sr had the piss in a J-cloth and under the tap before Veronica had time to turn from the cooker to see what had happened.

Jimmy Sr studied his shoulder.

—That's grand.

—Change it, said Veronica.

—Not at all, said Jimmy Sr. —It's grand.

Tracy came back in with the pup clinging to the front of her jumper.

—Look it. He's hangin' on by himself.

—What're yis goin' to call him? Jimmy Sr asked.

—Don't know.

—Wha' abou' Larry Gogan? said Jimmy Sr.

He looked across at Jimmy Jr, but Jimmy Jr didn't know he was being slagged.

—That's stupid, said Linda.

—It's thick, said Tracy.

—No, it's not, said Jimmy Sr. —Listen. How many —?

—Call him Anthrax, said Jimmy Jr.

—They will not, said Veronica.

—Look it, said Jimmy Sr when he'd stopped laughing. —If yis call him King or Sultan or somethin' like tha' an' yis shout ou' his name half the dogs in Barrytown'll come runnin' at yis; d'yeh see? But if yis call him Larry Gogan he's the only one that'll come to yis cos there's not all tha' many dogs called Larry Gogan as far as I know.

—It's an excellent name, said Jimmy Jr.

The girls looked at each other.

—Okay, said Linda. —We were goin' to call it Whitney.

—It's a boy, said Jimmy Sr, laughing.

—Yeah.

—Your name's Larrygogan, Tracy told the pup.

Larrygogan didn't look all that impressed.

—Howyeh, Larrygogan.

—Will yis do a message for me, girls?

—Yeah, said Linda.

Jimmy Sr always paid them for messages.

—Get a choc-ice for your mammy —

—I want a Toblerone as well, said Veronica.

—Certainly, Veronica, said Jimmy Sr. —A choc-ice an' a small Toblerone, an' you can have choc-ices as well.

—Can we just have the money?

—No way. Choc-ices. An', come here, I want to see yis eatin' them.

—Not till they've had their tea, said Veronica.

—Did yis hear tha'? said Jimmy Sr. —An' get one for Darren an' as well.

—Wha' abou' me? said Jimmy Jr.

—Buy your own.

—Aaah! He's gorgeous!

Sharon had just walked in and seen Larrygogan.

—There's Sharon, said Jimmy Sr. —D'yeh want a choc-ice, Sharon?

—Yeah thanks, Daddy.

—A celery one, is it?

—Very funny, I don't think.

Sharon patted Larrygogan.

—God, he's only a skeleton.

—He's from Ethiopia, said Jimmy Jr.

Jimmy Sr, Linda, Tracy and Sharon laughed but Veronica didn't. They heard a bang from above them. The bunk beds in the boys' room had hopped. Les and Darren were fighting.

—STOP THA', Jimmy roared at the ceiling. ——There.

He gave three pound notes to Linda.

—We'll bring Larrygogan, said Tracy.

Sharon laughed.

—Is tha' wha' yis're callin' him?

—That's righ', said Jimmy Sr.

He winked at her.

—Don't bring him, he told the twins. —He'll have to have his shots. If yis bring him ou' before he has his shots he'll catch diseases.

—What's shots?

—Injections.

—Ah no!

—They're nice injections. They don't hurt. They'll tickle him. An' annyway, if he doesn't have them he'll catch all sorts o' diseases. An' then Jimmy here'll catch them off o' him an' give them to all his pals.

—I'll wear a johnny, Jimmy Jr whispered to Sharon.

—Oh Jesus! Sharon laughed.

—Take it easy, said Jimmy Sr.

—Right, said Veronica. —Ready. Sharon, give me a hand here.

—Dash, girls, Jimmy Sr told the twins.

And they did.

And Larrygogan fell into the sink.

* * *

On the Tuesday morning after Larrygogan joined the family, in the middle of week eleven, Sharon got an awful fright when she was climbing out of bed, just waking up. Her period had started.

—Oh no! ——Oh God ——

She'd been robbed.

But then she remembered: she'd read in the book that this could happen. It wasn't a real period. It probably wasn't a real period.

She stayed at home in bed and waited. She lay there, afraid to move too much. She tried to remember the Hail Mary but she couldn't get past Hello Be Thy Name, and anyway, she didn't believe in it, not really; so she stopped trying to remember the rest of it. It was just something to do. She wanted to turn on her side but she was afraid to. She just lay there and she started saying Please please please please all the time to herself. She kept everything else out of her mind. She concentrated on that.

—Please please please please.

The book was right. It didn't last long. It wasn't the same. It wasn't a real period at all. She was still pregnant.

*   *   *

—Aah! Jaysis!!

Veronica put the skirt on the table and got up to see what was wrong in the hall. But before she got to the door Jimmy Sr came hopping into the kitchen with one of his leather slippers in his hand.

—What happened? said Veronica.

—The dog's after shitein' in the fuckin' hall an' I fuckin' stood in it, that's wha' happened.

—On the floor?

—No. On the fuckin' ceilin'. Jesus!

He hopped over to the sink and put the slipper under the tap. Veronica came back from the hall.

—It's comin' off alrigh', Jimmy Sr told her.

—What about the carpet?

—The twins'll be cleanin' tha', don't worry. An' the sink here.

—It's disgusting, said Veronica.

Jimmy Sr inspected the slipper. It was grand and clean again. He threw it on the floor and stepped into it.

—Ah, he's only a pup, he said.

—He'll have to go. They're not training him properly.

—Give him a chance, Veronica. You'll be expectin' the poor little bollix to eat with a knife an' fork next.

Veronica gave up and got back to the skirt. She was just finishing Linda's and then she had Tracy's to do.

Jimmy Sr saw the twins out in the back. They were trying to get Larrygogan to catch a burst plastic football but Larrygogan was having problems staying upright. If the ball

27

landed on him Jimmy Sr thought it would kill him. The grass needed cutting. Larrygogan kept disappearing in it.

Jimmy Sr opened the back door.

—Get in here, you-is!

* * *

Sharon woke up and she knew she was going to be sick.

She was hunched down at the toilet bowl. There was sweat, getting cold, on her face. She shivered. More puke, not much now —hardly any —rushed into her mouth.

—Yu —hh ——!

It dropped into the water and she groaned. She squeezed her eyes shut. She wiped them, then her nose, and her eyes again. She stood up carefully. She was cold.

—Are yeh alrigh' in there, Sharon?

It was Jimmy Sr.

—Yeah, she said. —Ou' in a minute.

—No hurry, Jimmy Sr assured her. —I was in already.

Sharon rubbed her arms. A wave of horribleness ran through her.

She gagged. She really felt terrible, and weak. She leaned against the wall. It was cool; nice. She knew she wasn't going to be sick again. This morning.

She thought about nothing.

—Are yeh stayin' in there, or wha'?

It was the other Jimmy.

Sharon unlocked the door.

—What's your fuckin' hurry? she said.

Jimmy Jr looked at her face.

—Wha' were you drinkin' last nigh'? he asked.

Sharon passed him. She was going back to bed. That was where she wanted to be.

The twins looked at her.

—Are yeh not well, Sharon? Linda asked her.

—No, said Sharon.

—That'll be the flu, said Linda.

Tracy agreed with her.

—There's a bug goin' around, she said. —Cover yourself up properly.

They went downstairs to get a cup of tea and a bit of dry toast for Sharon. Sharon rubbed her legs. Only her forehead was cold now.

Well, she was pregnant now alright. She pressed her stomach gently: still nothing, but she was on her way. She smiled, but she hoped to God it wasn't going to be like this every morning.

When she took her hand away from her stomach —probably because she didn't feel sick any more —she noticed that her skin there was kind of sore, a bit like sunburn but not nearly as bad. She pressed again: yeah, the same. She tried her tits.

—Ouw! —

She'd been half-aware of that soreness for a few days but it was only now, because she'd just been sick, that she paid proper attention and linked it to being pregnant. They used to get a bit sore before her periods, but now —God, it was all starting to happen.

She'd have to tell her friends now; no, soon.

Jesus.

Tracy ran in.

—Ma said to say if yeh keep not goin' to work you'll be sacked an' jobs don't grow on trees.

—Tell her I'll be down in a little while.

Linda came in. She had Larrygogan with her.

—Larrygogan wants to say Howyeh.

She brought him over to Sharon's bed so he could lick Sharon's face. Sharon lifted her head for him.

—Hiyeh, Larry.

He stared at her. Linda put him right up to Sharon's nose.

—Kiss her, she said.

Nothing happened.

—Kiss her, will yeh.

—Give us a kiss, Larry, said Sharon.

—Daddy said we're to call him his whole name so he'll know who he is, said Tracy.

—He kisses us, Linda told Sharon. —Tracy, doesn't he?

—Yeah.

—He doesn't really know me yet, that's all, said Sharon. —Bring him back down now, will yeh.

—Okay. Come on, Larrygogan.

Linda ran out.

—Tracy, will yeh tell Mammy I'm gettin' up now, said Sharon.

She sat up.

—Ah, said Tracy. —Do yeh not have the flu?

—No.

—Ah janey.

She sounded very disappointed.

—Wha'? said Sharon.

—I wanted to catch it off yeh, an' so did Linda.

Sharon laughed.

—Why?

—Don't want to do the majorettes annymore, said Tracy. —It's stupid.

—I thought yis liked it.

—No. We used to. But it's stupid.

—Why is it? Sharon asked.

—It's just stupid, said Tracy. —She won't let us be in the front.

—Why won't she?

—Don't know. ——She hates us. It's prob'ly cos Daddy called her a wagon at tha' meetin'.

Sharon laughed. She got out of bed.

—He didn't really call Miss O'Keefe a wagon, she told Tracy. —He was only messin' with yeh.

Tracy continued.

—Nicola 'Malley's in the front an' she's nearly always droppin' her stick an' me an' Linda only drop ours sometimes.

—It's not fair, sure it's not, said Sharon.

Tracy followed her into the bathroom.

—No, she agreed. —The last time Nicola 'Malley threw her stick through the fuckin' window.

Sharon nearly bit the top off her toothbrush.

—Tracy!

—It just came ou'. ——She did though, Sharon.

—An' is she still in the front row?

—Yeah. It's not fair. ——An' the music's stupid.

They were back in the bedroom.

—What is it? Sharon asked.

—Don't know. A woman singin' Moll-ee My Irish Moll-ee, or somethin'. Miss O'Keefe thinks it's brilliant but it's thick.

Jimmy Sr shouted from downstairs.

—Are yeh ready for a lift, Sharon?

—Nearly.

—Make it snappy, will yeh.

He strolled back into the kitchen. Veronica was the only one still in there.

—Cummins is comin' ou' to have a look at the plasterin' this mornin' an' we've still got one o' the rooms to do, Jimmy Sr told her.

—Did you mention about a job for Leslie to him? Veronica asked him.

—Not yet. I will but. Today.

—Mm, said Veronica.

—I will now, Jimmy Sr assured her. —Scout's honour. Is he up yet?

—Not at all.

—We'll have to put a stop to tha'.

He picked up his sandwiches.

—Wha' are they? he asked.

—It's a surprise.

—It's not Easy Slices, is it?

Veronica turned to the sink.

—Is it? It is. Ah Jaysis, Veronica! How many times —!?

Linda came in from the back.

—Does the dog like sandwiches, does he? Jimmy Sr asked her.

And he lobbed the tinfoil pack out the door into the back garden.

* * *

It was the thirteenth week of Sharon's pregnancy and the middle of May, but it was cold.

—It's fuckin' freezin', said Jimmy Sr, and he was right.

Any time now, Sharon knew, and the real swelling would start. But she kept putting off telling the girls. Twice in the last week she'd gone down to the Hikers and she was definitely going to tell them. But she didn't. She couldn't.

She could've told them she was pregnant. That wouldn't have been too bad, not all that embarrassing really. But it was the big question that would come after that —WHO? —that was what she couldn't face.

But she'd have to tell them sooner or later and, judging by what she'd been reading, it would have to be sooner.

She struggled through her book. She read forward into the weeks ahead. Parts of it terrified her. She learned that the veins in her rectum might become painful. She was sure she felt a jab just after she'd read that.

She might get varicose veins. Or nosebleeds. Better than iffy rectum veins, she thought. Oedema sounded shocking. She could see herself filling up with water and bouncing around. Larrygogan would claw her and she'd have a puncture.

All these things were bad but when she read about eclampsia she went to the toilet and got sick. She shook and shivered for ages after it. She read it again: protein in the urine —blurred vision —severe headaches —hospital —swelling of face and fingers —she read it very slowly this time ——eclampsia ——convulsions ——coma ———death. She was going to catch it, she knew it. She always got the flu and colds when they were going around. She didn't mind the protein in her urine, or even the blurred vision so much. It was the word Convulsions that got to her.

So much could go wrong. Even when it was okay there seemed to be nothing but secretions and backache and constipation. And she'd thought there was no more to it than getting bigger and then having it and maybe puking a few times along the way.

Still, nothing was going wrong so far. The book said there might be vomiting in the mornings, and there was —not every morning though. The book said her breasts would be tender. She'd always thought that that was another word for Good when you were talking about meat but she looked for it in Darren's dictionary and that was what her tits were alright. They were still the same colour though. Her nipples were the same colour as well, although it was hard to tell for sure. They changed colour every day in the bathroom mirror.

She started doing sit-up exercises and touching her toes when she got home from work. They'd make carrying the extra weight easier. As well as that the exercises helped to squeeze water from the pore spaces in her blood vessels.

But the book didn't say what happened to the water after that. Sometimes she forgot about the exercises though, and sometimes she just didn't feel like it; she was too knackered. Anyway, she was tall and quite strong and she always walked straight, so she didn't think the exercises mattered that much. She really did them because she wanted to do everything right, and the book said she should do them.

She was drinking a lot of milk. She was eating oranges. She kept reminding herself to go to a chemist's and get vitamin pills. She was eating All-Bran four times a week.

—What's tha' stuff like, Sharon? Jimmy Sr asked her one morning she'd the time to eat her breakfast sitting down.

—Horrible, said Sharon.

—Does it work?

—Sort of, yeah.

—Ah well, that's the main thing, isn't it? ——You don't need it, sure yeh don't?

He was talking under the table to Larrygogan.

She kept eating the celery and the carrots. The right food was hard and boring and it took ages to eat but Sharon thought she was doing things the right way, and that pleased her. And excited her. She felt as if she was getting ready, packing to go somewhere —for good. And that frightened her a bit.

She felt her stomach. It was harder and curved, becoming like a shell or a wall.

She'd definitely have to tell the girls.

*　*　*

It was Tuesday morning. It was raining. There was war going on downstairs in the kitchen.

Linda and Tracy put the table between themselves and their mother.

—What's wrong now? Jimmy Sr wanted to know.
—Can a man not eat his bit o' breakfast in peace?
—It's stupid, Ma, said Linda.
—Yeah, said Tracy.
—Mammy! said Veronica.
—Mammy, said Linda. —It's stupid.
—I don't care, said Veronica. —I spent hours making those skirts for you two little rips —
—They're stupid, said Linda.
She hadn't meant to say that. She knew she'd made a mistake but she hated those skirts, especially her own one.
Veronica roared.
—Aaah!
The hours she'd wasted; cutting, clipping, sewing, making mistakes, starting again.
Jimmy Sr threw his knife and fork onto the plate.
—Wha' kind of a fuckin' house is this at all? he asked the table.
He looked at Veronica. She was deciding if she'd throw the marmalade at the twins.
—A man gets up in the mornin', said Jimmy Sr. —an' —an' —
—Oh shut up, said Veronica.
—I will not shut up, said Jimmy Sr. —A man gets up —
—Hi-dee-hi, campers, Jimmy Jr greeted them all when he came into the kitchen.
—Fuck off, Jimmy Sr shouted.
Jimmy Jr looked down at Jimmy Sr.
—Do yeh not love me annymore, Daddy?
—Yeh sarcastic little prick, yeh, said Jimmy Sr. —If —
—Stop that language, said Veronica.
—I'm only startin', said Jimmy Sr.
—Miss O'Keefe said yeh should be ashamed of yourself, Linda told Jimmy Sr.
This interested Jimmy Sr.

—What? said Veronica.

Darren came in and sat down and started eating Sugar-Puffs.

—They're ours, said Tracy.

—So? said Darren.

—When did, eh, Miss O'Keefe say tha' to yis? Jimmy Sr asked.

—Last week.

—Yeah, said Tracy.

—WHY did she say it? Veronica asked.

—Yeh took the words righ' ou' of me mouth, said Jimmy Sr.

—When Tracy said wha' you said, Linda told him.

—You said it as well! said Tracy.

—I did not!

—Girls, girls, said Jimmy Sr. —Wha' happened? Exactly. He looked at Veronica. She looked away.

—She told everyone to say wha' our mammies an' our daddies said to each other tha' mornin'.

—Oh my God! said Veronica.

Jimmy Jr started laughing. Darren was listening now as well.

—An' it was real borin' cos they were all sayin' things like Good mornin' dear an' Give us the milk. ——An' Tracy said wha' you said to Mammy.

She looked at Tracy. Tracy was going to kill her.

Veronica sat down.

—An' would yeh by any chance remember wha' I said to your mammy? Jimmy Sr asked.

——Yeah.

—Well? What was it?

—Yeh pointed ou' the window ——at the rainin' —

She pointed at the window.

—An' then yeh said ——

Jimmy Jr laughed. He remembered.

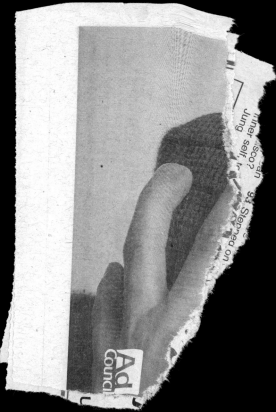

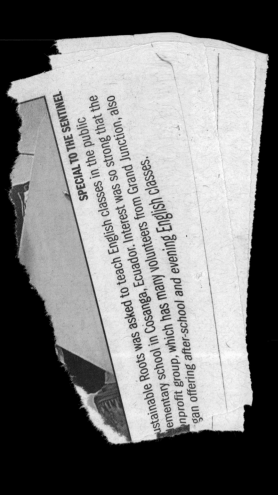

SPECIAL TO THE SENTINEL

...ustainable Roots was asked to teach English classes in the public ...ementary school in Cosanga, Ecuador. Interest was so strong that the ...nprofit group, which has many volunteers from Grand Junction, also ...gan offering after-school and evening English classes.

—Go on, said Jimmy Sr.

—You said It looks like another fuck of a day.

Jimmy Jr howled. So did Darren. Jimmy Sr tried not to.

Veronica put her hands to her face and slowly dragged her fingers down over her cheeks. Her mouth was open.

—Oh sweet Jesus, she said then, to no one.

Sharon came in.

—Hiyis, said Sharon. —What're yis laughin' at?

—There's Sharon, said Jimmy Sr. —How are yeh, Sharon?

—Grand.

—Good. ——Good.

He started laughing.

—Serves her righ', the nosey brasser.

Jimmy Jr, Darren and the twins laughed. Jimmy Sr grinned at Veronica.

—Listen, he said to the twins. —If she asks yis again today tell her —

—No!

That was Veronica.

The Rabbittes laughed.

—What're yis laughin' at? Sharon still wanted to know.

—You, said Jimmy Jr.

Sharon gave him a dig.

—Mammy, you can give the skirts to the poor people, said Linda.

This tickled Jimmy Sr.

—What's this? said Jimmy Jr.

—None o' your business, said Jimmy Sr.

—What poor people? said Veronica.

—The Ethiopians, said Jimmy Jr.

Linda and Tracy giggled.

—I think that's a lovely idea, Linda, said Jimmy Sr. —Fair play to yeh.

—Stop encouraging them, said Veronica.

—Stop? said Jimmy Sr, shocked. —Well now, I hope Miss O'Keefe doesn't hear abou' this. My God, wha'. The twins's mother won't let them show a bit o' charity to those less fortunate than —

—Stop that!

Darren was in stitches. He loved it when his da talked like that.

—I'm sure there's a couple o' piccaninnies —

—Daddy!

The boys laughed, cheering on Jimmy Sr. The twins were still giggling, and looking at their mammy.

——in a refugee camp somewhere that'd love a couple o' red lurex majorette's dresses. An' the sticks as well.

—You're not fit to be a father, said Veronica.

—Not now maybe, Jimmy Sr admitted.

He patted his gut.

—I used to be though, wha'.

He winked at Veronica. She growled at him. Jimmy Sr looked at the boys and raised his eyes to heaven.

—Women, wha'.

He lowered the last of his tea. Then he heard something, a scraping noise.

—What's tha'?

—Larrygogan, said Tracy. —He wants to come in.

Linda opened the door. Larrygogan, even smaller than usual because his hair was stuck down by the rain, was standing on the step.

—Come on, Larrygogan, said Linda.

Larrygogan couldn't make it. He fell back twice. They laughed.

—The poor little sappo, said Jimmy Sr.

Linda picked him up and carried him in and put him down on the floor. He skidded a bit on the lino, then shook himself and fell over.

Then he barked.

The Rabbittes roared laughing. Jimmy Sr copied Larrygogan.

—Yip! Yip!

He looked at his watch.

—Oh good shite!

He was up, and grabbed his sandwiches.

—Are yeh righ', Sharon? ——Wha' are they, he asked Veronica.

—Corned beef.

—Yippee. ——Good luck now. See yeh tonigh'.

He wondered if he should kiss Veronica on the cheek or something because they were both in a good mood at the same time. But no, he decided, not with the boys there. They'd slag him.

—Da, can I've a bike for me birth'y? Darren asked him.

—Yeh can in your hole, said Jimmy Sr.

—Ah, Da!

—Forget it, Sunshine.

Jimmy Sr waited for Sharon to go out into the hall first.

—Good girl.

He followed her.

—Hang on a sec, he said, at the front door.

He gave Sharon the keys of the van.

—Let yourself in.

Les thought it was a heart attack. He tried to scream, but he couldn't.

Jimmy Sr's hand was clamped tight over Les's face. He waited till Les was awake and knew what was happening.

—That's the front o' me hand, Jimmy Sr told Les.

He pushed Les's head deeper into the pillow.

—If yeh don't get up for your breakfast tomorrow like I told yeh you'll get the back of it. D'yeh follow?

Jimmy Sr took his hand off Les's face.

—Now get up, yeh lazy get, an' don't be upsettin' your mother.

He stopped at the door.

—I want to talk to you tonigh', righ'.

Downstairs, Jimmy Jr and Darren heard a snort. They looked and saw their mother crying. It was terrible. She was wiping tears from her eyes before they could get to her cheeks.

But she wasn't crying. She was laughing. She tried to explain why.

—They're not —

She started laughing again.

—They're not corned beef at all.

A giggle ran through her, and out.

—They're Easy Slices.

They didn't know what she was on about but they laughed with her anyway.

* * *

Sharon was in bed. She'd decided: tomorrow. She'd been half-thinking of doing it tonight but then Jackie had come in with the big news: she'd broken it off with Greg. So they'd had to spend the rest of the night slagging Jackie and tearing Greg apart. It'd been brilliant crack.

So Jackie would be there when she told them all tomorrow. That was good because the two of them always defended one another when the slagging got a bit serious. She was going to tell the rest of the family first, after the tea —that would be easy —and then the girls, later in the Hikers.

That was it, decided. But she wasn't a bit sleepy now. She had been when she got into bed but once she'd made up her mind she was wide awake again.

What was she going to tell them; how much? Only that she was pregnant. But what was going to happen after that, and what they were going to ask and say, and think; that's what was worrying her.

—Go on, Sharon, tell us. Who was it?

There was no way she was going to tell them that. If they ever found out ——God, she'd kill herself if that happened, she really would. She couldn't think of a good enough lie to tell them, one that would stop them from asking more questions. She could say she didn't know who he was but they wouldn't believe her. Or if they did, if Sharon told them she'd been so pissed she couldn't remember, they'd help her remember and they wouldn't give up till they'd found someone. —Was it him, Sharon, was it? And if Sharon said, No, it wasn't him, they'd say, —How d'yeh know if yeh can't remember? It must've been him then.

She'd just have to tell them that she wasn't going to tell them.

But they'd still try and find out.

She didn't blame them. She'd have been the same. It was going to be terrible though. She wouldn't be able to really relax with them any more.

—There's Keith Farrelly.

—Yeah.

—He's a ride, isn't he?

—He's alrigh'.

—D'yeh not like him?

—He's alrigh'.

—I thought that yeh liked him.

—Fuck off, will yeh. It wasn't him.

It was going to be fuckin' terrible.

She felt a bit lonely now. She'd have loved someone to talk to, to talk to nonstop for about an hour, to tell everything to. But —and she was realizing this now really —there was no one like that. She'd loads of friends but she only really knew them in a gang.

It hadn't been like that in school. Jackie had been her

best friend for years but now that was only because she saw her more often than the others, not because she knew her better. She'd never have been able to tell Jackie all about what had happened. They'd often talked about fellas; what he did and how he did it and that sort of thing, but that had only been for a laugh; messing. They hadn't spoken seriously about anything to do with sex since —since Sharon had her first period. Or they'd pretended it wasn't serious. It was always for a laugh. Giggling, roaring, saying things like, —I swear, Jackie, I was scarleh. ——She really had something to be scarlet about now and it wasn't even a little bit funny. And she couldn't tell it to Jackie. And anyway, Jackie had been going with Greg until last weekend so she hadn't seen her that much since —she knew the date —the twentieth of February.

That was always the way when one of the gang was going with someone. She'd disappear for a while, usually a couple of months, and come back when one of them broke it off. She'd come back to the pub and they'd all be delighted to see her and she'd have to slag the fella —it always happened —about how he was always farting, or how he kept trying to tear the tits off her, or how his tongue always missed her mouth in the dark and he slobbered all over her make-up (Sharon giggled as she thought of that one. Yvonne Burgess had said that about a fella in the army who'd gone off to the Lebanon without telling her. —I hope he's fuckin' kilt, said Yvonne. —By an Arab or somethin'. D'yeh know wha' his ma said when I phoned? He's gone to the Leb. The Leb! I thought it was the name of a pub or somethin' so I said to her, D'yeh know wha' time he'll be back at? I'm tellin' yis now, I swear, I was never so mortified in —my —life. I wasn't. And they'd screamed laughing), and after that it was like she'd never been gone. It was back to normal till the next time they went to Saints or Tamangos or one of the places in town and one of them got off with a fella she liked and disappeared again for another couple of months. She'd often read in magazines and she'd seen it on television where it said that women friends were closer than men, but Sharon didn't think they were. Not the girls she knew. ——Anyway, if she couldn't tell Jackie the whole lot —and she couldn't —then she couldn't tell anyone.

She'd have to be careful and not get too drunk again so she wouldn't blabber, and make sure she wasn't caught looking at him and try not to vomit if anyone mentioned his name and Jesus, it was going to be terrible.

If they ever found out! She tried to imagine it. But all she could do was curl up and groan. It was ——

Years ago —four years ago —when she'd been a modette, she'd gone with this young fella called Derek Cooper who spent all of his money on clothes and then never washed them and was dead now, and the two of them missed the last DART from town so they got the last bus instead. She'd been really pissed. She was only a kid then. She'd gotten the money she got for doing the pre-employment in school the day before so she'd been loaded. She paid for his drink as well. Anyway, she was pissed and she fell asleep on the bus and she woke up and she'd wet herself and she had to tell him and she made them stay on till the last stop, Howth. It was horrible remembering it. Even now. She'd never been able to laugh about it. She'd nearly been glad when she found out that Derek Cooper had been killed in that crash, but she'd made herself cry.

But this —this was far worse than that.

Sharon didn't even bother closing her eyes. There was no point. She waited for the time to get up.

It was mad, but she wished she'd had sex a lot more often. Doubts about the father would have been very comforting; lovely. But the last time she'd done it with a fella she'd really liked —who'd turned out to be a right fuckin' bastard —was six months before.

Before ——Jesus!

She was glad she didn't remember much about it. The bits she did remember were disgusting. It wasn't a moving memory, like a film. It was more like a few photographs. She couldn't really remember what happened in between. She'd been really drunk, absolutely paralytic. She knew that because she remembered she'd fallen over on her way back from the toilets. She bumped into loads of people dancing. It was the soccer club Christmas do, only it was on in February because they weren't able to get anywhere nearer to Christmas. She'd made it back to her table and she just sat there, trying not to think about getting sick. She remembered Jackie was asking her was she alright. Then it was blank. Then she was by herself at the table. Jackie was getting off with a fella in front of her. That was Greg. She could remember the song: The Power of Love, the Jennifer Rush one. She wasn't sure if it was then or after but she was very hot, really sweating. She was going to be sick. She rushed and pushed over the dance floor, past the toilets, outside because she wanted cold air. It was blank again then for a bit but she knew that she didn't puke. The air had fixed her. She was leaning against the side of a car. She was looking at the ground. It was just black gravel so she didn't know why she was looking at it; maybe because she'd thought she was going to get sick earlier. Anyway, she was shivering but she didn't move; go back in. Pity. She couldn't move really. Then there was a hand on her shoulder. —Alrigh', Sharon? he'd said. Then it was blank and then they were kissing rough —she wasn't really: her mouth was just open —and then blank again and that was it really. She couldn't remember much more. She knew they'd done it —or just he'd done it —standing up because that was the way she was in the next bit she remembered; leaning back against the car, staring at the car beside it, her back and arse wet through from the wet on the door and the window and she was wet from him too. She was very cold. The wet was colder. He was gone. It was like waking up. She didn't know if it had happened. She wanted to be at home. At home in bed. Her knickers were gone. And she was all wet and cold there. She wanted to get into bed. She went straight home. She staggered a lot, even off the path. She wanted to sleep. Backwards. To earlier. She was freezing but she didn't go back for her jacket.

Jackie brought it and her bag home for her the day after.

—What happened yeh?

—Jesus, I was pissed, Jackie, I'm not jokin' yeh. I just came home. I woke up in me clothes.

—Yeh stupid bitch yeh.

—I know.

She'd wondered a few times if what had happened could be called rape. She didn't know.

That was as much as she remembered. She wished she didn't remember more. ——When he sat down white skin poked out from between the buttons of his shirt.

There was one more thing she remembered; what he'd said after he'd put his hand on her shoulder and asked her was she alright.

—I've always liked the look of you, Sharon.

Sharon groaned.

The dirty bastard.

*　*　*

Les was nearly crying. So was Veronica.

—Shut up! The lot o' yis! said Jimmy Sr.

—You started it, Jimmy Jr reminded him.

—Good Jesus!!

—I'm goin' to smash your fuckin' records, Les told Jimmy Jr.

This time Veronica slapped him hard across the head.

45

—Wha'!?

—Don't Wha' me, said Veronica, and she slapped him again. —Don't think you can stroll in and out of here when you feel like it and shout language like a —like a knacker.

She drew her hand back, Les ducked, and then she slapped him.

Linda and Tracy were giggling.

—Don't start, youse! Jimmy Sr roared at them.

—You never hit THEM, do yeh? said Les.

He was crying now.

—I'm not takin' this.

He slammed the back door.

Jimmy Sr was going after him.

—Leave him out there, said Veronica. —It's going to rain in a minute. That'll bring him back.

Jimmy Sr couldn't leave it just like that. He'd lost, in front of Darren, the twins, Sharon —them all. He was the head of the fuckin' house!

—Come here, you, he said to Jimmy Jr. —If you ever behave like that again in this house yeh can pack your belongin's. Your groovy clothes an' your shampoo an' —an' your bras an' yeh can fuck off to somewhere else, righ'. Is tha' clear?

—I don't know, said Jimmy Jr. —I'll have to discuss it with my solicitor.

A laugh burst out of Darren. He'd have loved the neck to say something like that.

—Don't YOU start!

Darren stopped.

And Jimmy Sr felt a bit better.

—Now, he said. —Sharon has a bit o' news for yis.

Veronica started laughing.

—Sorry, she said. —I can't help it.

—Darren, said Jimmy Sr. —We live in a mental home.

Darren laughed.

—Sorry, Sharon, said Veronica. —Go on, love.

Sharon grinned at Veronica. She looked at the twins when she spoke.

—I'm goin' to be havin' a baby.

*   *   *

Jimmy Sr and Veronica were alone in the kitchen. Jimmy Sr was having the cup of tea he always had before he went out.

—These yokes aren't as nice as they used to be, said Jimmy Sr. —Sure they're not?

He put the rest of the Jaffa Cake on the table.

—That doesn't stop you eating them.

—I didn't say they weren't nice, Veronica. Wha' I said was —

—Right. Right. I agree with you.

—Are yeh tired, Veronica?

—Mm, said Veronica.

—Will yeh go on up to the bed?

—Mm.

—That's the place to be. ——It went well, didn't it?

—I suppose it did, said Veronica.

—They took it very well, I thought.

—Ah Jimmy, for Christ's sake. What did you expect? Did you think the girls would be outraged or something?

——No.

He grinned at her.

—I didn't think they'd go tha' wild. Poor Sharon won't have any peace now. Inside —

He nodded at the door.

—watchin' the telly there, Sharon yawned an' Tracy asked her was she havin' the baby. ——Tha' Jimmy fella's a righ' pup though. He said somethin' to Sharon, yeh know, cos I saw her hittin' him. She gave him a righ' wallop.

—They get on very well, those two.

—I don't know, said Jimmy Sr.

He sighed.

—You were exactly like him, said Veronica.

—Veronica, please. It's been a rough day. Now, lay off.

—Remember that Crombie you had?

—No.

—You do so. You used to keep it spotless. Except for your dandruff.

—I didn't have dandruff!

—Excuse me, you did so. My Uncle Bob used to say that we needed a Saint Bernard dog to find everyone after you'd been in the house.

Jimmy Sr laughed.

—He was an oul' bollix, tha' fella. A right oul' bollix. I bought tha' fucker a brandy at the weddin', I did. ——Annyway, we didn't have those special shampoos. Timotei. So mild you can wash your hair as often as yeh like! As if yeh didn't have better things to be doin' than washin' your fuckin' hair all day. As often as yeh like!

—What happened that coat?

—I don't know! I threw it ou'.

—You did not. After you bought it you stopped trying to get me to go into the fields with you. It was the best contraceptive ever invented, that coat.

—Veronica!

—That's what they should give every young lad these days. A nice new coat.

Jimmy Sr laughed.

They said nothing for a while. Then Veronica spoke.

—Jimmy.

—Yes, Veronica?

—Do you not think —? —You'll probably shout at me for saying it. ——I think we should tell the twins that what Sharon did was wrong.

—Wha'?

—No, listen. I don't want to turn them against her or anything —

—An' the baby, remember.

—Yes, I know that. But —

—Wha'?

—I think we should tell them. Without, you know. We should tell them that they should only have babies when they're married.

—They wouldn't understand wha' you were on abou'.

—Oh they would, you know.

—Maybe they would. ——It's a bit young but, isn't it? Wha' were yeh thinkin' o' tellin' them?

He was flicking fluff and specks off his jumper. That meant he was on his way out.

—Do you not think we should? Veronica asked him.

—Well, whatever you think yourself, Veronica, said Jimmy Sr. —They'd only laugh at me. I'm only their da. Anyway, it'd sound better comin' from a woman, wouldn't it? ——Maybe leave it till they're a bit older.

—But by then —

She couldn't finish. There was no tidy way of saying what she thought. She gave up. Maybe she'd talk to Sharon about it.

Jimmy Sr was standing up, ready to go. But he didn't want to leave Veronica unhappy.

—Times've changed, Veronica, he said.

—I suppose so, said Veronica. —But do we have to keep up with them?

Jimmy Sr didn't like questions like that.

—D'yeh want to come? he asked Veronica.

—Ah no.

—Up to the bed?

—Mm; yeah.

—That's the place. See yeh later.

—Bring your Crombie. It might rain.
—Ha fuckin' ha.

*   *   *

—How much did it cost yeh, Jackie? Yvonne asked.
She dipped two wetted fingers into her crisp bag and dredged it for crumbs.
—Fifteen pound, ninety-nine, said Jackie.
—Really? said Yvonne. —That's brilliant, isn't it?
—Is it hand wash, Jackie? said Mary.
—Yeah, it is.
—It's very nice now.
—Thanks.
Yvonne wiped her fingers on the stool beside her.
Sharon saw this as she walked over to join them so she parked herself on the stool opposite Yvonne.
—Hiyis, she said.
—Hiyeh, Sharon.
—Ah howyeh, Sharon.
—Hiyis, said Sharon.
—Are they new, Sharon?
—No, not really.
A lounge boy was passing. Sharon stopped him.
—A vodka an' a Coke, please, she said.
—Don't bother abou' the Coke, Sharon, said Jackie. —I've loads here, look it.
—Okay. Thanks, Jackie. A vodka just, she told the lounge boy.
—Anyway, Jackie, said Mary.
The real business of the night was starting.
—Will yeh be seein' Greg again?
—Tha' prick! said Jackie.
They laughed.
Jackie had given Greg the shove the Saturday before

—or so she said anyway —in one of those café places in the ILAC Centre, after he'd accused her of robbing the cream out of his chocolate eclair. —An' I paid for the fuckin' thing! she'd told them the night before.

She was in good form tonight as well. She tapped the table with her glass.

—If he was the last man on earth I wouldn't go with him.

She took a fair sip from the glass.

—I'd shag the Elephant Man before I'd let him go near me again, the prick.

They roared.

—Yis should've seen him with that fuckin' eclair. I was so embarrassed, I was scarleh, I'm not jokin' yis, I was burnin'. In his leather jacket an' his fuckin' keys hangin' off his belt, yeh know, givin' the goo goo eyes to a fuckin' eclair. It was pat'etic, it was.

—Were yeh goin' to break it off annyway? Sharon asked her.

—Yeah, said Jackie. —I was thinkin' about it alrigh'. I was givin' the matter, eh, my serious consideration.

They laughed.

—Then when I saw him sulkin'; Jesus!

—He was very good lookin' though, wasn't he? said Yvonne. —Very handsome.

—Not really, said Jackie. —Not when yeh got up close to him. D'yeh know what I mean?

—Beauty is only skin deep, said Mary.

—It wasn't even tha' deep, Mary, Jackie told her. —He had loads o' little spots on his chin. Tiny little ones now. Millions o' them. You only noticed them when you were right up against him, an' then you'd want to throw up. ——There was nothin' under the leather jacket really. That's all he was now that I think of it.

Jackie sighed and took a slug from her glass.

—A leather jacket. ——He was thick as well.

—Come here, Jackie, said Mary. —Was he passionate?

—No, said Jackie. —But he thought he was. Yeh know? He was just a big thick monkey.

—Lookin' for somewhere to stick his banana, wha', said Yvonne.

They screamed.

—Yvonne Burgess!

Sharon wiped her eyes.

—He stuck his tongue in me ear once, Jackie told them when they'd settled down again. —An', I'm not jokin' yis, I think he was tryin' to get it out the other one. I don't know what he fuckin' thought I had in there.

She laughed with them.

—He licked half me brains ou'. Like a big dog, yeh know.

They roared.

Jackie waited.

—His sense o' direction wasn't the best either, d'yis know what I mean?

They roared again.

—Jesus!

—Jackie O'Keefe! You're fuckin' disgustin'!

—Wha'?

More vodkas and Cokes and a gin and a tonic were ordered. And crisps.

Then Sharon told them her bit of news.

—I'm pregnant, did I tell yis?

Mary laughed, but the others didn't. Then Mary stopped.

—Yeah, well, said Sharon. —I am.

—She's fuckin' serious, said Yvonne.

No one said anything for a bit. Sharon couldn't look anywhere. The others looked at one another, their faces held blank. Sharon picked up her glass but she was afraid to put it to her mouth.

Then Jackie spoke.

—Well done, Sharon, she said.

—Thanks, Jackie.

She put the glass down. She was starting to shake. Suddenly she couldn't breathe in enough air to keep her going.

—Yeah, Sharon. Congrats, said Mary.

—Thanks, Mary.

—Well done, Sharon, said Yvonne. —Yeh thick bitch yeh.

Then they all started laughing. They looked at one another and kept laughing. Sharon was delighted. They were all blushing and laughing. The tears were running out of her and the snot would be as well in a minute. She took up her bag from the floor to look for a hankie.

The laughing died down and became fits of the giggles. They all blew their noses and wiped their eyes.

—Jesus though, Sharon, said Jackie, but she was grinning.

Sharon reddened again.

—I know, she said. —It's terrible really.

Some questions had to be asked.

First an easy one.

—How long are yeh gone, Sharon? Yvonne asked her.

—Fourteen weeks.

They converted that into months.

—Jesus! Tha' long? said Mary.

They looked at Sharon.

—You don't look it, said Yvonne.

—I do, said Sharon.

—I won't argue with you, said Yvonne. —You're the expert.

They screamed.

—I'm only messin', said Yvonne.

Sharon wiped her eyes.

—I know tha'.

—You look the same, said Mary.

—I'll start gettin' bigger in a few weeks.

—Well, said Jackie, —you can start hangin' round with someone else when tha' happens. No fellas'll come near us if one of us is pregnant.

They laughed.

—Sharon, said Yvonne. —Who're yeh havin' it for?

Your fat da, thought Sharon.

—I can't tell, she said. —Sorry.

She looked at her drink. She could feel herself going red again.

—Ah, Sharon!

She grinned and shook her head.

—Meany, said Jackie.

Sharon grinned.

—Give us a hint.

—No.

—Just a little one.

Nothing.

—Do we know him?

—No, said Sharon.

—Ah Sharon, go on. Tell us.

—No.

—We won't tell annyone.

—Leave Sharon alone, said Jackie. —It's none o' your fuckin' business. Is he married, Sharon?

—Oh Jesus! said Mary.

—No, said Sharon.

She laughed.

—You're scarleh. He must be.

—He's not. I swear. He's not —

—Are yeh gettin' married? Mary asked.

—No. I mean —I mean I don't want to marry him.

—Are yeh sure we don't know him?

—Yeah.

—Is he in here?

—Jesus, said Jackie. —If we don't know him he isn't here. An' anyway, would you do it with annyone here?

—I was only fuckin' askin', said Yvonne.

She looked around. The lounge was fairly full.

—You're righ' though, she said. —It was a stupid question. Sorry for insultin' yeh, Sharon.

—That's okay.

—Serious though, Sharon, said Mary. —Do we really not know him?

—No. I swear to God.

—I believe yeh, thousands wouldn't, said Yvonne.

—Where did yeh meet him?

—Ah look, said Sharon. —I don't want to talk about it annymore; righ'?

—Let's get pissed, will we? said Jackie.

—Ah yeah, said Sharon.

—Hey! Jackie roared at the lounge boy. —Get your body over here.

They laughed.

The lounge boy was sixteen and looked younger.

—Three vodkas an' two Cokes an' a gin an' tonic, said Jackie. —Got tha'?

—Yeah, said the lounge boy.

—An' a package o' crisps, said Yvonne.

—Ah yeah, said Sharon. —Two packs.

—Do yeh have anny nuts? Mary asked him.

—Jesus, Mary, yeh dirty bitch yeh!

They screamed.

—I didn't mean it tha' way, said Mary.

The very red lounge boy backed off and headed for the bar.

Yvonne shouted after him.

—Come back soon, chicken.

—Leave him alone or he'll never come back, said Jackie.

—Who's goin' to sub me till Thursday? said Yvonne.

—Me, said Sharon. —I will. A tenner?

—Lovely.

—He'll be nice when he's older, won't he? said Mary.

—Who? The lounge boy?

Jackie looked over at him.

—He's a bit miserable lookin'.

—He's a nice little arse on him all the same, said Yvonne.

—Pity there's a dickie bow under it, said Jackie.

They stopped looking at the lounge boy.

—Annyway, Sharon, said Jackie. —What's it like? Are yeh pukin' up in the mornin's?

—No, said Sharon. —Well, yeah. Only a couple o' times. It's not tha' bad.

—I'd hate tha'.

—Yeah. It's bad enough havin' to get up without knowin' you're goin' to be vomitin' your guts up as well.

—It's not tha' bad, said Sharon.

—Are you goin' to give up work? Mary asked her.

—I don't know, said Sharon. —I haven't thought about it really. I might.

—It's nice for some, said Yvonne. —Havin' a job to think abou' givin' it up.

—Ah, stop whingin', said Jackie.

—I wasn't whingin'.

—Would you really like to be doin' wha' Sharon does, would yeh? Stackin' shelves an' tha'?

—No.

—Then fuck off an' leave her alone.

—Are you havin' your periods or somethin'?

—Yeah, I am actually. Wha' about it?

—You're stainin' the carpet.

The row was over. They nearly got sick laughing. The lounge boy was coming back.

—Here's your bit o' fluff, Mary, said Sharon.

—Ah stop.

—Howyeh, Gorgeous, said Jackie. —Did yeh make your holy communion yet?

The lounge boy tried to get everything off the tray all at once so he could get the fuck out of that corner.

He said nothing.

—Wha' size do yeh take? Yvonne asked him.

The lounge boy legged it. He left too much change on the table and a puddle where he'd spilt the Coke. Mary threw a beer-mat on top of it.

—Jesus, Sharon, said Jackie. —I thought you were goin' to have a miscarriage there you were laughin' so much.

—I couldn't help it. —Wha' size d'yeh take.

They started again.

—I meant his shirt, said Yvonne.

They giggled, and wiped their eyes and noses and poured the Coke and tonic on top of the vodka and gin.

—Are yeh eatin' annythin' weirdy? Mary asked Sharon.

—No, said Sharon.

—Debbie ate coal, Jackie told them.

—Jesus!

—I wouldn't eat fuckin' coal, said Sharon.

—How d'you eat coal? Mary asked.

—I don't know! said Jackie. —The dust, I suppose.

—My cousin, Miriam. Yeh know her, with the roundy glasses? She ate sardines an' Mars Bars all squashed together.

—Yeuhh! Jesus!

—Jesus!

—That's disgustin'.

—Was she pregnant? said Jackie.

—Of course she ——Fuck off, you.

They all attacked their drinks.

—He won't come back, said Jackie. —We'll have to go up ourselves.

—Come here, Sharon, said Yvonne. —Was it Dessie
Delaney?

—No!

—I was on'y askin'.

—Well, don't, said Sharon. —I'm not tellin', so fuck off.

—Was it Billy Delaney then?

Sharon grinned, and they laughed.

Sharon put her bag under her arm.

—Are yeh comin', Jackie?

—The tylet?

—Yeah.

—Okay.

Jackie got her bag from under the table. They stood up.
Sharon looked down at Yvonne and Mary.

—Me uterus is pressin' into me bladder, she told them.

—Oh Jesus!

They roared.

* * *

—Annyway, said Bimbo. —I gave him his fiver an' I said,
Now shag off an' leave me alone.

—A fiver! said Paddy. —I know wha' I'd've given the
cunt.

—I owed him it but.

—So wha'? said Paddy. —Tha' doesn't mean he can
come up to yeh outside o' mass when you're with your mot
an' your kids an' ask yeh for it.

—The kids weren't with us. Just Maggie an' her mother.

—Jimmy!

—Wha'? said Jimmy Sr from the bar.

—Stick on another one, said Paddy. —Bertie's here.

Bertie saluted those looking his way and then sat down
at the table with Paddy and Bimbo.

—There y'are, Bertie, said Bimbo.

—Buenas noches, compadre, said Bertie.

—How's business, Bertie? said Paddy.

—Swings an' roundabouts, said Bertie. —Tha' sort o' way, yeh know.

—Tha' seems to be the story everywhere, said Bimbo. —Doesn't it?

—Are you goin' to nigh' classes or somethin'? said Paddy.

Bertie laughed.

—Ah fuck off, you now, said Bimbo. —Every time I open me mouth yeh jump down it.

—There's plenty o' room in there annyway, said Bertie, —wha'.

They heard Jimmy Sr.

—D'yis want ice in your pints?

He put two pints of Guinness down on the table, in front of Paddy and Bimbo. There was a little cocktail umbrella standing up in the head of Bimbo's pint.

Jimmy Sr came back with the other two pints.

—How's Bertie?

—Ah sure.

—It's the same everywhere, isn't it? said Paddy.

Bertie sniggered.

Bimbo was spinning the umbrella.

—Mary Poppins, said Jimmy Sr.

—Who? said Bimbo. —Oh yeah.

He held the umbrella up in the air and sang.

—THE HILLS ARE A—

Paddy squirmed, and looked around.

—LIVE WITH THE SOUND O' —no, that's wrong. That's not Mary Poppins.

—It was very good, all the same, said Jimmy Sr.

—It fuckin' was, alrigh', Bertie agreed. —Yeh even looked like her there for a minute.

Bimbo stuck his front teeth out over his bottom lip, and screeched.

—JUST A SPOONFUL OF SHUGEH —
HELPS THE MEDICINE ——GO DOWN —
THE MEDICINE ——GO DOW —
                              WOWN —
THE MEDICINE ——GO DOWN —
—Are yeh finished? said Paddy.
—Do your Michael O'Hehir, said Jimmy Sr.
—Ah, for fuck sake, said Paddy. —Not again. All o' them horses are fuckin' dead.
—Weuahh!
That was Bertie.
—Jesus! ——fuck!
He gasped. His mouth was wide open. He shook his face. He was holding his pint away from his mouth like a baby trying to get away from a full spoon.
He pointed the pint at Jimmy Sr.
—Taste tha'.
—I will in me hole taste it. What's wrong with it?
—Nothin', said Bertie.
And he knocked back a bit less than half of it.
—Aah, he said when he came up for air. —Mucho good.
Bimbo put the umbrella into his breast pocket.
—Wha' d'yeh want tha' for? said Paddy.
—Jessica, said Bimbo. —She collects them. Maggie brings all hers home to her.
Paddy looked across to Jimmy Sr and Bertie for support. Jimmy Sr grinned and touched his forehead.
—Oh yeah, said Bertie.
He'd remembered something. He picked the bag he'd brought in with him off the floor and put it on his lap.
—You don't follow Liverpool, said Paddy.
—It's Trevor's, said Bertie. —I had to take all his bukes an' copies ou' of it cos I'd nothin' else. There was a lunch in the bottom of it an', fuckin' hell. Did yis ever see blue an' green bread, did yis?

—Ah fuck off, will yeh.

—The fuckin' meat. Good Christ. It stuck its head ou' from between the bread an' it said, Are The Tremeloes still Number One?

He put his face to the opening and sniffed.

—Yeh can still smell it. The lazy little bastard. Annyway, Jimmy, he said. —Compadre mio. How many bambinos have yeh got that are goin' to school.

—Eh ——three. Why?

Bertie took three Casio pocket calculators in their boxes out of the bag.

—Uno, dos, tres. There you are, my friend. For your bambinos so tha' they'll all do well for themselves an' become doctors.

—Are yeh serious? said Jimmy Sr.

He picked up one of the calculators and turned it round.

—Si, said Bertie.

He explained.

—There's a bit of a glut in the calculator market, yeh know. I took three gross o' them from a gringo tha' we all know an' think he's a fuckin' eejit —

—An' whose wife does bicycle impressions when he isn't lookin'?

—That's him, said Bertie. —I gave him fuck all for them. I was laughin' before I'd the door shut on the cunt, yeh know. Only now I can't get rid o' the fuckin' things. No one wants them. I even tried a few o' the shops. Which was stupid. But they were gettin' on me wick. I can't live with failure, yeh know. So I'm givin' them away. Righ', Bimbo. How many do you need?

—Five, said Bimbo.

—Five!?

—He only has four, said Jimmy Sr. —He wants one for himself.

Bimbo held up his left hand. He pointed to his little finger.

—Glenn.

He moved on to the next finger.

—Wayne.

The middle one.

—Jessica.

—Okay okay, said Bertie. —There'll be six by the time you've finished.

He dealt the boxes out to Bimbo.

—Uno, dos, tres, four, five.

—Thanks very much, Bertie.

—No problem, said Bertie. —See if yeh can get them to lose them, so I can give yeh more. I still have two gross in intervention. A fuckin' calculator mountain. ——Cal-cul-ators! We don't need your steenking cal-cul-ators! I speet on your cal-cul-ators! ——Paddy?

—Wha'?

—How many?

—I don't want your charity.

Bertie, Jimmy Sr and Bimbo laughed. Paddy was serious, but that made it funnier.

—None o' those kids he has at home are his annyway, said Jimmy Sr.

The stout in Bimbo's throat rushed back into his mouth and bashed against his teeth.

—My round, compadres, said Bertie.

He stood up.

—Three pints, isn't that it? he said.

They looked up at him.

—Do yeh want me charity, Paddy, or will yeh stay on your own?

—Fuck off.

—Four pints, said Bertie.

Jimmy Sr and Bimbo laughed and grinned at each other. Paddy spoke.

—Fuck yis.

Bertie took two more calculators out of the bag.

—For my amigos, the barmen.

When he got back from the bar Bimbo had one of the calculators out of its wrapper.

—The round costs five pound, forty-four, he told them.

—Go 'way! said Jimmy Sr.

—That's very fuckin' dear all the same, isn't it? said Bimbo.

—It was just as dear before yeh got the calculator, said Bertie.

—I know, I know tha'. It's just when yeh see it like tha' in black an', eh, silvery grey it makes it look worse. ——I think annyway.

—My Jaysis, said Paddy.

He looked at Bertie.

—Fuckin' hell, said Bimbo. —If there was six of us the round'd cost —

—Put it away, Bimbo, for fuck sake, said Jimmy Sr.

—I've got two kids in school, Paddy told Bertie.

—Is tha' righ'? said Bertie.

—Yeah.

—Well, I hope they're good at their sums, said Bertie. —Cos they're not gettin' anny calculators.

—Young Sharon's after gettin' herself up the pole, Jimmy Sr told them.

He rubbed his hands and picked up his pint.

—Is tha' YOUR Sharon, like? said Bimbo.

—That's righ', said Jimmy Sr. —Gas, isn't it?

—One calculator for Sharon, said Bertie, and he passed one across to Jimmy Sr, and then another one. —And one for the bambino. A good start in life.

—She's not married, said Bimbo.

—I know tha'! said Jimmy Sr.

—Is tha' the tall girl tha' hangs around with Georgie Burgess's young one? Paddy asked.

—That's righ', said Jimmy Sr.

—Is she gettin' married? said Bimbo.

—No, said Jimmy Sr. —Why should she? They've more cop-on these days. Would you get married if you were tha' age again these days?

—I think I'm goin' to cry, said Bertie.

—I'd say I would, yeah, said Bimbo.

—What're yeh askin' him for, for fuck sake? said Paddy. —He brings home little umbrellas for his kids. He goes to meetin's. He brought his mot to the flicks last week.

—Only cos her sister's in hospital, said Bimbo. —She usually goes with her sister, he told Jimmy Sr. —The Livin' Daylights, we went to. The James Bond one.

—Is it anny good?

—Ah it is, yeah. It's good alrigh'. ——There's a lovely lookin' bird in it. Lovely.

—Oh, I've seen her, said Bertie.

—Isn't she lovely?

—Oh si. Si. A little ride.

—Ah no. She's not. She's the sort o' bird, said Bimbo, —that yeh wouldn't really want to ride. D'yeh know wha' I mean?

—No.

Paddy shook his head and looked at Bertie, and grinned.

—Is she a cripple or somethin'?

—No! said Bimbo. —No. ——She's TOO nice, yeh know?

—You'd give her little umbrellas, would yeh?

—Fuck off, you, said Bimbo.

Bertie put a calculator in front of Bimbo.

—Give her tha' the next time yeh see her.

—Who did the damage? Paddy asked Jimmy Sr.

—We don't know, to tell yeh the truth, said Jimmy Sr. —She won't tell us.

—Well, you'd want to fuckin' find ou', said Paddy.

—What's it you who it is? said Bimbo.

—I couldn't give a fuck who it is, said Paddy. —It's Jimmy. I'm not goin' to be buyin' food for it, an' nappies an' little fuckin' track suits. Jimmy is.

—I am in me hole, said Jimmy Sr. —Hang on though. Maybe I will be.

He thought about it.

—So wha' though. I don't care.

—Good man, said Bimbo.

—An' she'll have her allowance, said Bertie.

—Will she? said Jimmy Sr. —I don't know. I s'pose she will. I don't care.

—Of course yeh don't, said Bimbo. —Such a thing to be worryin' abou'! Who's goin' to pay for it!

—Will yeh listen to him, said Paddy. —The singin' fuckin' nun.

—Fuck off.

—I believe Gerry Foster's young fella's after puttin' some young one from Coolock up the stick, Bertie told them.

—Wha'? said Jimmy Sr. —Jimmy's pal? What's this they call him? Outspan.

—Yeah. Him.

Jimmy Sr laughed.

—I'd say tha' made his hair go curly.

—Is he marryin' her? Bimbo asked.

—Yes indeed, said Bertie. —A posse came down from Coolock. Mucho tough hombres. They hijacked the 17A. Take us to Barrytown, signor.

They laughed.

—I believe the poor fucker's walkin' around with half an 8 iron stuck up his arse.

—Where's he goin' to be livin'?

They knew the answer they wanted to hear.

—Coolock, said Bertie.

—There's no need for all tha' fuss, said Jimmy Sr, when they'd stopped laughing. —Sure there's not?

—Not at all, said Bimbo. —It's stupid.

Bertie agreed.

—Thick, he said.

—It's only a baby, said Bimbo. —A snapper.

—Doctor Kildare, Bertie said to Paddy.

—That's it, said Paddy.

—Fuck off, youse, said Bimbo.

—I wouldn't want Sharon gettin' married tha' young, said Jimmy Sr.

—She's her whole life ahead of her, said Bimbo.

—Unless she drinks an iffy pint, said Bertie.

—Annyway, said Jimmy Sr.

He lifted his glass.

—To Sharon, wha'.

—Oh yeah. Def'ny. Sharon.

Bertie picked up his pint.

—To the Signorita Rabbeete that is havin' the bambino out of wedlock, fair play to her.

He gave Jimmy Sr another calculator.

—In case it's twins.

—Stop, for fuck sake.

Bimbo filled his mouth, swallowed, filled it again, swallowed and put his glass back on its mat.

—Havin' a baby's the most natural thing in the world, he said.

Jimmy Sr loved Bimbo.

—D'you know wha' Sharon is, Jimmy? Said Bimbo.

——Wha'?

—She's a modern girl.

—Oh good fuck, said Paddy.

*　*　*

Sharon was lying in bed.

Well, they knew now. They'd been great. It'd been great.

She was a bit pissed. But not too bad. She shut her eyes, and the bed stayed where it was.

She'd never laughed as much in her life. And when Yvonne had pinched the lounge boy's bum, the look on his face. And Jackie's joke about the girl in the wheelchair at the disco. It'd been brilliant.

Then, near closing time, they'd all started crying. And that had been even better. She didn't know how it had started. Outside, they'd hugged one another and said all sorts of stupid, corny things but it had been great. Mary said that the baby would have four mothers. If she'd said it any other time Sharon would have told her to cop on to herself but outside in the car-park it had sounded lovely.

Then they'd gone for chips. And Jackie asked the poor oul' one that put the stuff in the bags how she kept her skin so smooth.

Sharon laughed —

Soon everyone would know. Good. She could nearly hear them.

—Sharon Rabbitte's pregnant, did yeh hear?

—Your one, Sharon Rabbitte's up the pole.

—Sharon Rabbitte's havin' a baby.

—I don't believe yeh!

—Jaysis.

—Jesus! Are yeh serious?

—Who's she havin' it for?

—I don't know.

—She won't say.

—She doesn't know.

—She can't remember.

—Oh God, poor Sharon.

—That's shockin'.

—Mm.

—Dirty bitch.

—Poor Sharon.

—The slut.

—I don't believe her.

—The stupid bitch.

—She had tha' comin'.

—Serves her righ'.

—Poor Sharon.

—Let's see her gettin' into those jeans now.

Sharon giggled.

Fuck them. Fuck all of them. She didn't care. The girls had been great.

Mister Burgess would know by tomorrow as well. He probably knew now. He might have been up when Yvonne got home. ——Fuck him too. She wasn't going to start worrying about that creep.

She couldn't help it though.

*　*　*

—There's Stephen Roche, said Darren.

—Wha'? said Jimmy Sr.

He looked over his Press.

—Oh yeah.

The Galtee cheese ad was on the telly.

—That's a brilliant bike, Da, look.

—No, said Jimmy Sr, back behind the paper.

—Ah, Da!

—No.

Jimmy Sr put the paper down.

—I'll tell yeh what I will do though, he told Darren.
—I'll buy yeh a box o' cheese. How's tha'?

Darren wouldn't laugh.

—What's on now? said Jimmy Sr.

He was sitting between Veronica and Sharon on the couch. He nudged Veronica.

—Leave me alone, you.

Jimmy Jr stuck his head into the room.

—Are yeh finished with the paper?

—No, said Jimmy Sr. —What's on, Sharon?

—Top o' the Pops, said Sharon.

—Oh good shite! said Jimmy Sr. —Where's the remote?

Sharon was getting up.

—Where're yeh off to now? he asked her nicely.

—The toilet.

—Again!? Yeh must be in a bad way, wha'.

Sharon sat down again. She whispered to Jimmy Sr.

—Me uterus is beginnin' to press into me bladder. It's gettin' bigger.

Jimmy Sr turned to her.

—I don't want to hear those sort o' things, Sharon, he said. —It's not righ'.

He was blushing.

—Sorry, said Sharon.

—That's okay. Who's tha' fuckin' eejit, Darren?

—Can you not just say Eejit? said Veronica.

—That's wha' I did say! said Jimmy Sr.

Darren laughed.

Veronica gave up.

—Da, said Darren.

—No, yeh can't have a bike.

Darren got up and left the room in protest. That left Jimmy Sr and Veronica by themselves.

—There's Cliff Richard, said Jimmy Sr.

Veronica looked up.

—Yes.

—I'd never wear leather trousers, said Jimmy Sr.

Veronica laughed.

Jimmy Sr found the remote control. He'd been sitting on it.

—He's a Moonie or somethin', isn't he? he said as he stuck on the Sports Channel. —And an arse bandit.

—He's a Christian, said Veronica.

—We're all tha', Veronica, said Jimmy Sr. —Baseball! It's worse than fuckin' cricket.

He looked at it.

—They're dressed up like tha' an' chewin' gum an' paint on their faces, so you're expectin' somethin' excitin', an' wha' do yeh get? Fuckin' cricket with American accents.

Jimmy Jr stuck his head round the door.

—Finished with the paper yet?

—No.

—You're not even lookin' at it.

—It's my paper. I own it. Fuck off.

Jimmy Sr switched again; an ad for a gut-buster on Sky.

—Jesus!

—You've got the foulest mouth of anyone I ever knew, Veronica told him. —Ever.

—Ah lay off, Veronica.

The front door slammed and Darren walked past the window.

—It's not his birthd'y for months yet, said Jimmy Sr. —Sure it's not?

—A bike's much too dear for a birthday, said Veronica.

—God, yeah. He has his glue ——What's tha' ANCO thing Leslie's signed up for, again?

—He's only applied, said Veronica. —He doesn't know if he'll get it. ——Motorbike maintenance.

—Wha' good's tha' to him? He doesn't have a motorbike.

—I don't know, said Veronica. —It lasts six months, so there must be something in it.

—But he doesn't have a motorbike. An' he's not gettin' one either. No way.

—You don't have to have a car to be a mechanic, said Veronica.

—That's true o' course, said Jimmy Sr. —Still, it doesn't sound like much though.

—It's better than what you got him.

—That's not fair, Veronica.

—He says he'll be able to fix lawn-mowers as well.

—We'll have to buy one an' break it so.

—Ha ha.

—He might be able to do somethin' with tha' alrigh', said Jimmy Sr. —Go from door to door an' tha'.

—Yes, said Veronica.

—Get little cards done, said Jimmy Sr. —With his name on them.

—Yes, said Veronica. —That sort of thing.

—Leslie Rabbitte, lawn-mower doctor.

—Ha ha.

—He won't get much business round here. Everyone gets a lend o' Bimbo's.

—He can go further.

—That's true. ——It'll get him up with the rest of us annyway. An' a few bob. ANCO pays them.

—Yes.

—The EEC, Jimmy Sr explained. —They give the money to ANCO.

—An' who gives the money to the EEC? Veronica asked.

—Em, said Jimmy Sr. —I've a feelin' we do.

—There now, said Veronica.

Jimmy Sr stayed quiet for a while. He switched back to the baseball.

—Look at tha' now, he said. —Your man there swingin'

71

the bat. You'd swear somethin' great was goin' to happen, but look it.

He switched through all nine channels, back to the baseball.

—There. He hasn't budged. It's fuckin' useless. What's tha' you're knittin'?

—A jumper.

—I don't like purple.

—It's not purple and you won't be wearing it.

—Who will?

—Me.

—Good. 'Bout time yeh made somethin' for yourself. You have us spoilt.

—And then you never wear them.

—I do so. What's this I have on?

—That's a Dunnes one.

—It is in its hole.

—Can I buy the paper then?

It was Jimmy Jr.

—No!

Veronica picked the paper off the floor.

—Here.

Jimmy Jr grabbed it.

—Thanks, Ma.

And he was gone.

Veronica turned to Jimmy Sr.

—Do you think I stitch St Bernard tags and washing instructions on the jumpers when I've finished knitting them?

—No, Veronica. I don't think that at —

Veronica grabbed the tag that was sticking up at the back of Jimmy Sr's jumper.

—What's that? she said.

—Take it easy! said Jimmy Sr. —You're fuckin' stranglin' me.

Linda and Tracy ran in.

—Get tha' dog out o' here, Jimmy Sr roared.

—Ah! —

—Get him ou'!

He pressed the orange button and the telly popped off.

—Yeh can always tell when it's comin' up to the summer, he said. —There's nothin' on the telly.

—There's never anything.

—That's true o' course. But in the summer there's absolutely nothin'.

He was restless now and it wasn't even half-seven yet. He said it before he knew he was going to.

—I suppose a ride's ou' of the question.

—Hang on till I get this line done, said Veronica.

—Are yeh serious?

—I suppose so.

—Fuckin' great, said Jimmy Sr. —It's not even dark yet. You're not messin' now?

—No. Just let me finish this.

Jimmy Sr stood up.

—I'll brush me teeth, he said.

—That'll be nice, said Veronica.

*　*　*

—It doesn't really show yet, said Jackie.

—It does! said Sharon. —Look.

Sharon showed Jackie her side.

Jackie was sitting on Linda and Tracy's bed while Sharon got out of her work clothes.

—Oh yeah, said Jackie. —You'd want to be lookin' though.

—Everyone's lookin', Jackie.

They laughed.

Sharon went over to Jackie.

—Put your hand on it.

Jackie did, very carefully.

—Press.

—Fuck off, Sharon, will yeh.

—Go on.

Jackie pressed gently.

—God, it's harder than I thought, she said. —Oh Jesus, somethin's movin'!

She took her hand away. Sharon giggled. Jackie put her hand back.

—It's funny, she said.

Then she took her hand down.

—Thanks, Sharon, she said.

Sharon laughed.

—I won't show yeh the state of me nipples, she said.

—Aah Jesus, Sharon!

—Ah, they're not tha' bad, said Sharon. —They're just a funny colour, kind of. I can't wear these jeans annymore, look.

—Why not? ——Oh yeah. Yeh fat bitch yeh.

—These are grand though. Where'll we go?

—Howth?

—Yeah. Get pissed, wha'.

—Yeah.

*   *   *

—Jaysis, Sharon, said Jimmy Sr as he moved over on the couch to make room for her. —You'll soon be the same shape as me, wha'.

*   *   *

—Sharon, let's touch the baby.

—No!

—Aah!

—Alrigh'. Quick but. Daddy's waitin' on me.

* * *

—There's an awful smell o' feet in here, said Jimmy Sr.
—It's fuckin' terrible.

—It's the dog, said Jimmy Jr.

—He's wearin' shoes an' socks now, is he? said Jimmy Sr. —Where is he?

—Ou' the back, said Darren.

Jimmy Sr, Jimmy Jr and Darren were in the front room, watching the tennis.

—It can't be him so, said Jimmy Sr. —An' it's not me.

—Don't look at me, said Jimmy Jr.

They both looked at Darren. He was stretched out on the floor. Jimmy Sr tapped one of his ankles.

—Get up there an' change your socks an' wash your feet as well. Yeh smelly bastard yeh.

—Ah Da, the cyclin's on in a minute.

—I amn't askin' yeh to amputate your feet, said Jimmy Sr. —I only want yeh to change your fuckin' socks.

—But the —

—Get ou'!

—Come here, said Jimmy Jr as Darren was leaving the room. —Don't go near my socks, righ'.

—I wouldn't touch your poxy socks.

—Yeh'd better not.

—It's those fuckin' runners he wears, said Jimmy Sr.

—Yeah, said Jimmy Jr.

—His feet can't breathe in them.

—Yeah.

—Who's your one?

—Gabriella Sabatini.

—Jaysis, wha'.

—She's only seventeen.
—Fuck off. ——Are yeh serious?
—Yeah.
—Is she winnin', is she?
—Yeah.
—Good.

* * *

—Jesus, I wouldn't like tha', said Yvonne. —Some dirty oul' bastard with a rubber glove.

—It was a woman, said Sharon.

—Yeah?

—Yeah. She was very nice. Doctor Murray. She was real young as well. It took bleedin' ages though.

—How long abou'? Mary asked her.

—Ages. Hours. Most of it was waitin' though. All fuckin' mornin', I'm not jokin' yeh. She said it was because of the cut-backs. She kept sayin' it. She said I should write to me TD.

—The stupid bitch, said Jackie.

They laughed.

—Ah, she was nice, said Sharon. —Come here though. I nearly died, listen. She said she wanted to know me menstrual history an' I didn't know what she talkin' abou' till she told me. I felt like a right fuckin' eejit. I knew what it meant, like, but I was —

—Why didn't she just say your periods? said Yvonne.

—Doctors are always like tha', said Mary.

—Menstrual history, said Jackie. —I got a C in that in me Inter.

They roared.

* * *

76

—Mammy, said Linda.

Tracy stood beside her.

—What? said Veronica.

—Me an' Tracy are doin' ballroom dancin'.

Veronica opened her eyes and sat up on the couch and put her feet back into her slippers.

—Ballroom dancing, she said. —Is that not a bit old-fashioned for you?

—No, it's brilliant, said Tracy.

—Yeah, said Linda.

—Where are my glasses? said Veronica.

She wanted to see the twins properly.

—There, look.

Both girls went to get Veronica's glasses for her but Veronica got to them first. She put them on.

—How much? she said.

—Nothin'!

—There's a competition, said Linda, ——an' that's ten pounds but it isn't on for ages.

—Well, I know you want something, said Veronica. —So you might as well tell me what it is.

—We have to have dresses.

—Oh God, said Veronica.

*   *   *

Sharon bought some pants with elastic waists, baggy things that would get bigger as she got bigger. She wouldn't have been caught dead in them if she hadn't been pregnant but now, when she looked at herself in them, she thought she looked okay. She'd have looked stupid and pathetic in what she usually wore. She was happy enough with her new shape. She walked as straight as she could although now and again she just wanted to droop.

She was sweating a lot. Like a pig sometimes. She knew

she would, but it was embarrassing one day when she was putting jars of chutney on a high shelf in work and she felt a chill and looked, and under her arms was wringing. She felt terrible. She didn't know if anyone else had seen but she wanted to go around and tell everyone that she'd washed herself well that morning. As far as she knew she had a choice: she could drink a lot and sweat or she could stop and become constipated. Some choice. She kept drinking and wore a jumper in work.

She looked at her face. Was it redder or was it just the light? She thought she looked as if she'd just been running.

She met Mister Burgess once. It wasn't a real meeting because she crossed the road to the shops when she saw him coming round the corner and she looked at the girls playing football on the Green while he went past. He just went past, and that was what she wanted.

* * *

Jimmy Sr got out of the house earlier than usual because Veronica was in her moods again. Anyway, they were all watching Miami Vice at home and he couldn't stand it. It was like watching a clatter of Jimmy Jr's pals running around and shooting each other.

Bimbo was with him.

—Now, Bimbo continued, —there mightn't be annythin' in this.

He took a mouthful from his new pint.

—That's grand. ——It's a bit embarrassin' really —

He waited till Jimmy Sr was looking at him.

——But I heard him talkin' abou' Sharon. Your Sharon, like, on Sunday. Yeh know the way they all come in after the mornin' match.

—An' take over the fuckin' place; I know. Wha' was he

78

sayin' abou' Sharon? Jimmy Sr asked, although he'd already guessed the answer.

———He said she was a great little ride.

——My God ——said Jimmy Sr, softly.

His guess had been way wrong.

—What a ——I'll crease the fucker. Would yeh say he's upstairs?

Bimbo was shocked.

—Yeh don't want to claim him here, he said. —You'd be barred.

He lifted his glass.

—An' me.

Jimmy Sr was breathing deeply.

—You're right o' course, he said. —That's wha' he'd want.

He whacked his glass down on the counter. It didn't break. He gripped the ashtray. The two barmen braced themselves for some kind of action.

He took his hand away from the ashtray.

Bimbo was appalled when he heard, then saw, that Jimmy Sr was crying.

—He'd no right to say tha', Bimbo, said Jimmy Sr.

—I know, said Bimbo.

—Just cos —

He snuffled.

In a way, Bimbo felt privileged, even though it was terrible. He knew that Jimmy Sr would never have cried in front of the other lads.

It had gone very quiet in the bar.

—Yeh wouldn't want to be listenin' to tha' fella, Bimbo told Jimmy Sr. —I only told yeh cos ——I'm not sure why I told yeh.

—You were righ', Bimbo, said Jimmy Sr.

—It's pat'etic really, said Bimbo. —A grown man sayin' things like tha'.

—Exactly.

—Just cos she's pregnant.

—Exactly.

—It's stupid.

—Yeah.

—It's not worth gettin' worked up abou'.

—Still though, said Jimmy Sr.

They looked around. There was no one looking at them. Bimbo put his glass down.

—Sure, that's wha' we were put down here for. To have snappers.

—You should know, said Jimmy Sr.

—Ah here.

—Two pints, chop chop, Jimmy Sr called.

Bertie came in.

—Three pints!

—Buenas noches, lads, said Bertie.

—There y'are, Bertie, said Bimbo.

—Howyeh, Bertie, said Jimmy Sr.

—The rain she pisses down, Bertie told them.

Something was still eating Jimmy Sr.

—Why did he say it THA' way? he asked Bimbo.

—Wha'? said Bertie.

—Nothin', said Jimmy Sr.

—Okay; be like tha'.

—I will.

—Fuck you, amigo.

—Go an' shite, amigo.

—Here's the pints, said Bimbo.

Jimmy Sr looked at them.

—Get back there an' put a proper head on them pints, he told Dave, the apprentice barman. —Jaysis.

*   *   *

Sharon wasn't asleep.

—Sharon, are yeh awake?

She didn't answer.

He didn't know which side of the room he should have been talking into. He hadn't been in here in eight years, the last time he'd wallpapered the room.

—Are you awake, Sharon?

—Daddy, said Sharon. —Is tha' you?

—Yeah.

—Daddy, is tha' you? said Linda.

—Yes, pet. Go back to sleep. I want to talk to Sharon.

—Daddy, is tha' you? said Tracy.

—Yes, pet, said Linda. —Go back to sleep.

They laughed and giggled.

—Will yeh come down to the kitchen for a minute, Sharon? said Jimmy Sr.

He was making a sandwich for himself when Sharon got downstairs.

She was worried. She'd never been called out of bed before.

—Yeh might as well have a cup o' tea now you're up, said Jimmy Sr.

—Okay.

—Good girl.

Jimmy Sr sat down. Sharon went back to the sink and filled the kettle.

—Is somethin' the matter? she asked.

—Not really, no, Sharon. ——It's just, I heard somethin' tonigh'. An' I wanted to warn yeh.

Then he started eating his sandwich, a lemon curd one.

Sharon turned off the tap.

—Warn me?

She was really worried now. The kettle was heavy enough to hide the shakes. She took it over to the socket, and then went back to wash two cups.

—Well, yeah, said Jimmy Sr. —Warn.

He took a drop of lemon curd off the table with his finger, thought twice about licking it and rubbed it into his trousers.

—Yeh know your man, George Burgess?

Sharon was facing the kitchen window. She leaned over the sink and coughed. She turned on the tap.

—Are yeh alrigh' there? said Jimmy Sr.

—Yeah. I'll be fine.

—I thought yis only did tha' sort o' thing in the mornin's.

——Sometimes in the night as well.

—Is tha' righ'? God love yis.

Sharon felt a bit better. He was being too nice. He didn't know anything.

—What abou' Mister Burgess? she said.

—Ah, he was sayin' things abou' yeh.

—Wha' was he sayin' about me?

—Not to me face. He wouldn't fuckin' want to. It was Bimbo tha' told me. He said ——He was sayin' things abou' you, bein' pregnant.

—So wha'?

—Good girl.

—Wha' did he say?

—Ah ——He said you were a great little ride. So Bimbo says annyway.

—Mister Reeves wouldn't make somethin' like that up.

—God no, not Bimbo. Never.

—An' who's your man Burgess callin' little? I'm bigger than he is.

Jimmy Sr laughed, delighted.

—That's righ'. You're not upset or annythin'?

—No!

She filled the cups and worked at the teabags with a spoon.

—Really, bein' called a ride is a bit of a compliment really, isn't it?

—Jaysis, said Jimmy Sr. —I don't know. ——Thanks.

He took his cup.

—I suppose it is.

He tried the tea.

—That's grand, good girl. ——Still though, he'd no righ' to be sayin' things like tha'.

—Sure, fellas —men —are always sayin' things like tha' abou' girls.

—Ah yeah, but. Not daughters though.

—Don't be thick, Daddy. All girls are daughters.

—Well, not my fuckin' daughter then.

—That's hypocritical.

—I don't give a fuck what it is, said Jimmy Sr. —He has young ones of his own. Tha' pal o' yours —?

—Yvonne.

—That's righ'. ——It's shockin'. Annyway, I'm not havin' some fat little fucker insultin' any of my family. Specially not you.

—You're my knight in shinin' armour.

—Don't start.

He grinned. So did Sharon.

—I just thought tha' I should tell yeh, yeh know, said Jimmy Sr.

—Thanks.

—No problem.

—I'm goin' back up now, righ'?

—Okay. Night nigh', Sharon.

Les got tired and cold waiting out the back for his da to go to bed so he filled his lungs and opened the back door.

—Good Jaysis! Where were you till now?

—Ou'.

Les got past Jimmy Sr, behind his chair. Standing up quickly was always a problem for Jimmy Sr.

—Get back here, you.

But Les didn't come back. Jimmy Sr heard the boys' bedroom door being opened and closed. He'd get him in the morning. He started looking for a few biscuits.

Larrygogan yelped in his sleep.

—Shut up, you, said Jimmy Sr.

Sharon heard the boys' door as well. She was deciding what to do about Mister Burgess. It was simple: she'd go over to his place and tell him to stop saying things about her or she'd tell Missis Burgess, or something. She didn't really know him but she thought that that would give him a big enough fright. Simple. Not easy though; no way. She hated the idea of having to go over and talk to him, and look at him; and him looking at her. Still though, she had to shut him up.

She'd do it tomorrow.

The stupid prick.

*　*　*

It was half-six and Sharon was home from work. She was standing on the Burgess's front step. She was afraid she was making a mistake but she rang the bell again before she could change her mind.

Pat Burgess slid back the aluminium door.

—Yeah?

—Is Mister Burgess there?

—Yeah.

—Can I see him for a minute?

—He's still havin' his tea.

—Only for a minute, tell him.

Sharon looked in while she was waiting. It was a small hall, exactly the same as theirs. There were more pictures in this one though, and no phone. Sharon could hear children and adult voices from the kitchen. She could see the side of

Missis Burgess's back because she was sitting at the end of the table nearest the door. Then she saw Missis Burgess's face. And then she heard her voice.

—Is it George you want, Sharon?

God! thought Sharon.

—Yes, please, Missis Burgess. Just for a minute.

She wanted to run. Jesus, she was terrified but she thought Mister Burgess probably was as well. The kitchen door closed for a second and when it opened again Mister Burgess was there. There was a napkin hanging from his trousers. He looked worried alright. And angry and afraid. And a bit lost.

Looking at him, Sharon felt better. She knew what she was going to say: he didn't. She wasn't disgusted looking at him now. She just couldn't believe she'd ever let him near her.

Mister Burgess came towards her.

—Yes, Sharon? he said. To Missis Burgess.

—I want to talk to you, Sharon said quickly when he got to the door.

He wouldn't look at her straight.

—Wha' abou'?

—YOU know.

—I'll see yeh later.

—I'll tell Missis Burgess.

Mister Burgess looked back into the hall. A lift of his head told her to come in.

—Come into the lounge, Sharon, he shouted. —Sharon's here abou' Darren.

—Hiyeh, Sharon.

It was Yvonne, from somewhere in the kitchen.

—Hiyeh, Yvonne, Sharon called back.

—See yeh later.

—Yeah, okay.

She walked into the front room. Mister Burgess shut the door. He was shaking and red.

—Wha' do yeh think you're up to, yeh little bitch, he hissed.

—Wha' d'yeh think YOU'RE up to, yeh little bastard?

He didn't hiss now.

—Wha'?

—Wha' were yeh sayin' about me to your friends? said Sharon.

—I didn't say ann'thin' to annyone.

It was an aggressive answer but there was a tail on it.

—You said I was a ride. Didn't yeh?

George Burgess hated that. He hated hearing women using the language he used. He just didn't think it was right. It sounded dirty. As well as that, he knew he'd been snared. But he wasn't dead yet.

—Didn't yeh? said Sharon.

—Are yeh mad? I did not.

—I can tell from your face.

It wasn't the first time he'd been told that. His mother had said it; Doris said it; everyone said it.

—I was only jokin'.

—I'm a great little ride.

The word ride made him snap his eyes shut.

—I didn't mean anny harm. I only —

—Wha' else did yeh say about me?

—Nothin'.

—Maybe!

—I swear. I didn't. On the Bible. I didn't say annythin'. Else.

She was nearly feeling sorry for him.

—Yeh stupid bastard yeh.

He looked as if he was being smacked.

She went on.

—You got your hole, didn't yeh?

He shut his eyes again. He got redder.

—Wha' more do yeh want?

—I swear on the Bible, Sharon, I didn't mean anny harm, I swear. True as God now.

—Wha' did yeh say?

—Ah, it was nothin'.

—I'll go in an' tell her.

He believed her.

—Ah, it was silly really. Just the lads talkin', yeh know.

Sharon knew that one step towards the door would get her a better explanation, so she took one.

—We —they —we were havin' a laugh, abou' women, yeh know. The usual. An' the young lads, the lads on the team, they were goin' on abou' the young ones from around here. ——An' that's when I said you were a —I said it.

He looked at the carpet.

—Yeh dope. Wha' did yeh say tha' for?

—Ah, I don't know.

He looked up.

—I was showin' off.

——Wha' else?

—Nothin', I swear. They laughed at me. Some o' them didn't even hear me. They'd never believe that I got me ——have —Off you.

He was looking at the carpet again.

—They thought tha' I was jokin'.

He jumped when the door was opened by Missis Burgess.

—There y'are, love, he roared at her.

—Hello, Sharon, said Missis Burgess.

—Hiyeh, Missis Burgess, said Sharon. —I was just tellin' Mister Burgess abou' Darren.

—That's righ', Mister Burgess nearly screamed.

—Is somethin' wrong with Darren?

—He has a bit of a cold just.

—A cold, said Mister Burgess.

—Maybe flu.

—We'll just have to hope he's better for Saturday, said Mister Burgess. —God knows, we'll need him.

—I didn't know there was flu goin' around, said Missis Burgess. —I hope there isn't, ——now. Will you tell your mammy I was askin' for her?

—I will, yeah, Missis Burgess.

—When are yeh due, Sharon? Missis Burgess asked.

—November. The end.

—Really? You look sooner. ——D'you want a boy or a little girl?

—I don't mind. A girl maybe.

—One of each, wha', said Mister Burgess.

Missis Burgess looked at Mister Burgess.

—I'm off to my bingo now, George.

—Good, said Mister Burgess. —That's great. Have you enough money with yeh, Doris?

—My God, he's offerin' me money! He's showin' off in front of you, Sharon.

Sharon smiled.

—Bye bye so, Sharon, said Missis Burgess.

—See yeh, Missis Burgess.

—Don't forget the grass, George.

—No, no. Don't worry.

—Remember to tell your mammy now, Missis Burgess told Sharon.

Then she was gone.

Sharon knew what he was going to say next.

—Phew, he said. —Tha' was close, wha'.

—It'll be closer the next time if yeh don't stop sayin' things abou' me.

—There won't be a next time, Sharon, I swear to God. I only said it the once. I'm sorry. ——I'm sorry.

—So yeh should be. ——I don't mind bein' pregnant but I do mind people knowin' who made me pregnant.

——So ——you're pregnant, Sharon?

—Fuck off, Mister Burgess, would yeh.

They stood there. Sharon was looking at him but he wasn't looking at her, not really. She wanted to smile. She'd never felt power like this before.

—Sorry, Sharon.

Sharon said nothing.

She was going to go now, but he spoke. His mouth was open for a while before words left it.

——An', Sharon —

He rubbed his nose, on his arm.

—Yeah?

—I never thanked yeh for —yeh know. Tha' nigh'.

He was looking at the carpet again, and fidgeting.

—I was drunk, said Sharon.

She wanted to cry now. She'd forgotten That Night for a minute. She was hating him again.

—I know. So was I. I'd never've ——God, I was buckled. ——Em —

He tried to grin, but he gave up and looked serious.

—You're a good girl, Sharon. We both made a mistake.

—You're tellin' me, said Sharon.

—Hang on a sec, Sharon, he said. —I'll be back in a minute.

He went to the door.

—Wait there, Sharon.

Sharon waited. She was curious. She wasn't going to cry now. She heard Mister Burgess going up the stairs, and coming down.

He slid into the room.

—That's for yourself, Sharon, he said.

He had a ten pound note in his hand.

Sharon couldn't decide how to react. She looked at the money.

She wanted to laugh but she thought that that wouldn't

be right. But she couldn't manage anger, looking at this eejit holding out his tenner to her.

—Do you think I'm a prostitute, Mister Burgess?

—God, no; Jaysis, no!

—What're yeh givin' me tha' for then?

—It's not the way yeh think, Sharon. Shite! ——Em, it's a sort of a present —

The tenner, he knew now, was a big mistake.

—Yeh know. A present. No hard feelin's, yeh know.

—You're some fuckin' neck, Mister Burgess, d'yeh know tha'?

—I'm sorry, Sharon. I didn't mean it the way you're thinkin', I swear. On the Bible.

He was beginning to look hurt.

—We made a mistake, Sharon. We were both stupid. Now go an' buy yourself a few sweets —eh, drinks.

Sharon couldn't help grinning. She shook her head.

—You're an awful fuckin' eejit, Mister Burgess, she said. —Put your tenner back in your pocket.

—Ah no, Sharon.

He looked at her.

—Okay, sorry ——You're a good girl. And honest.

—Fuck off!

—Sorry! ——Sorry. I'll never open me mouth about you again.

—You'd better not.

—I won't, I swear.

Then he remembered something.

—Oh yeah, he said.

He dug into his trousers pocket.

—I kept these for yeh. Your, em, panties, isn't tha' what yis call them?

He was really scarlet.

—Me knickers!

Sharon was stunned, and then amused. She couldn't help it. He looked so stupid and unhappy.

She put the knickers in her jacket pocket. Mister Burgess, she noticed, wiped his hand on his cardigan. She nearly laughed.

—Wha' were yeh doin' with them? she asked.

—I was keepin' them for yeh. So they wouldn't get lost.

He was purple now. His hands were in and out of his cardigan pockets. He couldn't look at her.

—Don't start again, said Sharon. —Just tell us the truth.

—Ah Jaysis, it was stupid really. Again. ——A joke —I was goin' to show them to the lads.

—Oh my —!

—But I didn't I didn't, Sharon! I didn't.

He coughed.

—I wouldn't.

Sharon went to the door.

—I've changed me mind, she said. —Give us the tenner. I deserve it.

—Certainly, Sharon. Good girl. There y'are.

Sharon took the money. She stopped at the door.

—Remember: if you ever say annythin' about me again I'll tell Missis Burgess wha' yeh did.

—Yeh needn't worry, Sharon. Me lips are sealed.

—Well —Just remember. ——Bye bye.

—Cheerio, Sharon. Thanks, ——very much —

She was a great young one, George decided as Sharon shut the door after her. And a good looker too. But, my God ——! He sat down and shook like bejaysis for a while. She'd do it; tell Doris. No problem to her. He'd have to be careful. Think but: he'd ridden her. And he'd made her pregnant. HE had.

—Jaysis.

He was a pathetic little prick, Sharon thought as she went back across the road to her house. He was pathetic. He wouldn't yap anymore anyway. He'd be too scared to.

*　*　*

Bertie put his pint down.

—Caramba! he said. —That's fuckin' lovely.

—It is alrigh', Bimbo agreed. —Lovely.

—Is it a new bike? Jimmy Sr asked Bertie.

—Nearly, yeah, said Bertie.

—Fuck off now, said Jimmy Sr. —How old is it?

—A few months only.

—Any scratches?

—Not at all, said Bertie. —It's perfect.

Bimbo shifted to one side and farted. They started laughing.

—My Jaysis, said Paddy. —You're fuckin' rotten.

—There's somethin' dead inside you, d'yeh know tha'? said Jimmy Sr, waving his hand in the air and leaning away from Bimbo.

Bimbo wiped his eyes with his fist.

—Yeh can smell it from here, said a voice from a distant corner.

That got them laughing again.

—They sound great in these chairs, Bimbo explained.

—Yeah, said Bertie. —Tha' stuff's great.

—Leatherette.

—Si.

—I don't believe I'm hearin' this, said Paddy.

—Ah fuck off, Paddy, said Jimmy Sr. —Annyway, it's your twist.

Jimmy Sr turned back to Bertie.

—Okay, he said. —You're on.

—Good, said Bertie. —Mucho good. Are yeh sure now you'll be able to get me the jacks?

—No problem to me.

—An' one o' those yokes for washin' your arse? A bidet.

—No problem.

—Wha' would yeh want one o' them for? Bimbo asked.

—For washin' your arse, yeh fuckin' eejit, said Paddy.

—Yeah, but wha' would yeh want to do tha' for? Bimbo wanted to know. —Puttin your arse wet back into your knickers.

—You're got a point there, said Jimmy Sr.

—It's a buyer's market, Bimbo, compadre mio, said Bertie. —My client he wants to wash his hole, so ——I'll wash it for him meself if he pays me enough. Fawn? he asked Jimmy Sr.

—Okay. No problem.

—What's fawn? Bimbo asked.

—The colour!

—Oh yeah.

—Jesus, said Paddy.

* * *

—Wha' did yeh say to him? Yvonne asked.

—I said I couldn't help it, said Sharon.

—He must be a righ' fuckin' bastard, said Jackie. —I know what I'd've told him.

—I said I couldn't help it if I had to keep goin' to the toilet. He blushed, yeh should've seen him. Just cos I said Toilet.

—Jesus, are yeh serious? He must be red all the time, is he?

—He's a fuckin' eejit, said Sharon. —He said it wasn't fair on the other girls. An' I said they didn't mind. They don't annyway. Most o' them prefer the check-out. Cos they can sit down. ——'Cept when it's really busy. But you'd swear stackin' shelves was a fuckin' luxury, the way he talked. That's all he is annyway. A shelf stacker in a suit. He's not a real manager at all. He's only one o' them trainee ones. Paddy in the bakery called him tha' to his face once, a shelf stacker in a suit. It was fuckin' gas.

—Is he good lookin', Sharon? Mary asked.

—Are yeh jokin' me! said Sharon. —Yeh know Roland the Rat? Well, he looks like him. Only not as nice.

They laughed.

—Jesus then, listen, said Sharon.

She'd remembered something else.

—He asked me why I wasn't wearin' me uniform, an' I—

She did it as she said it.

—stuck me belly out an' I said, It doesn't fit me. Yeh should've seen his face, I'm not jokin' yis.

They screamed.

—Ah, said Jackie. —The poor chap must've been embarrassed.

—Yeah, Sharon, said Mary. —You're mean.

They laughed again.

—Well ——said Sharon. —I was only standin' up for me rights.

—You were dead right, Sharon, said Yvonne. —Yeh should've stuck one o' your tits in his mouth as well.

—Jesus!!

They really screamed now.

—Oh look it, said Yvonne when they'd recovered. —There's your chap, Mary.

They looked across at the lounge boy.

Yvonne waved at him.

—Come here!

—Is he comin'?

————No.

They started laughing again.

*   *   *

A few Sundays after Sharon had sorted out George Burgess, at a quarter to seven, Jimmy Sr was standing in the bar jacks, tucking a bit of shirt back into his fly. The lads had all gone home for their tea and to bring their wives back later —because it was Sunday. Jimmy Sr was going home now himself to collect Veronica.

He decided to wash his hands. They'd installed a new hand dryer and he wanted to have a go on it.

He had his hands in under the dryer and was wondering how long more it would take when he saw George Burgess in the mirror, coming in. George walked behind Jimmy Sr and put his hand on his shoulder. He smiled at Jimmy Sr in the mirror.

—How's it goin', Jimmy? he said.

Jimmy Sr shrugged violently.

—Get your fuckin' hands off me, Burgess.

George was very surprised, and worried.

————What's wrong with YOU? he asked, still looking at the mirror.

—You know fuckin' well what's wrong with me.

Jimmy Sr turned.

—I haven't a clue, Jim, said George.

He stepped back a bit, to make room for Jimmy Sr.

—Don't start, said Jimmy Sr. —If you're goin' to start tha' then we'll go outside an' have it ou' now.

George hadn't been in a fight since 1959, in Bray. He'd lost it, and two of his teeth. And, he was only realizing it now that this was Sharon's father he was having a row with.

—Look, Jimmy, I don't know wha' you're talkin' abou' so you'll have to tell me.

—I'll tell yeh alrigh'. You were sayin' things abou' Sharon.

Jimmy Sr's face dared George to deny it.

—I said nothin' abou' Sharon, Jimmy. I —

Jimmy Sr gave George's chest a good dig. It was loud but not too hard; a warning.

—Yeh fuckin' did, pal, said Jimmy Sr. —Cos Bimbo heard yeh.

—I didn't mean anny harm, for fuck sake; it was only a joke —

Jimmy Sr thumped him again, harder. George stayed put. He wasn't going to let himself be pinned to the urinal wall. He'd his good suit on him.

—You've got it wrong, Jim.

—Wrong me bollix!

—Yeh have, I swear.

—Me bollix.

Jimmy Sr was pressing into George by now.

—Just cos the poor young one's pregnant, he said.

—Look —

George was up against the wall. He had to get up onto the step.

—Look, I'm sorry, Jimmy.

—Yeh'd fuckin' want to be.

—I am, I sw —

—Yeh should be ashamed of yourself, a man o' your age sayin' things abou' young girls like tha'.

—I know —

—Yeh bastard, yeh. —You're not worth hittin'.

That, thought George, was good news.

—I'm sorry, Jimmy. Really now. On the Bible. I was just messin' with the lads, yeh know.

—The lads! said Jimmy Sr. —Yeh sound like a fuckin' kid.

Jimmy Sr turned away and went to the door. He wanted to whoop. He'd won. He stopped at the door.

—Come here, you, he said. —If you ever say another word abou' Sharon again I'll fuckin' kill yeh. Righ'?

—Righ', Jimmy. I won't. Yeh needn't worry. I'm not, eh —

George looked like a beaten man. And that chuffed Jimmy Sr a bit more.

—An' come here as well, he said. —If yeh drop Darren off the team cos o' this I'll kill yeh as well.

—Jaysis, Jimmy, I'd never drop Darren!

*   *   *

Darren walked into the kitchen.

—Happy birthd'y, son.

—Happy birthday, Darren.

—Happy birth'y, Darren.

—Good man, Darren, said Jimmy Sr. —There y'are.

He handed Darren a thin cylindrical parcel.

—Wha' is it?

—It's your birthd'y present, Jimmy Sr told him.

—It's not a bike.

—I know tha', said Jimmy Sr.

—What is it?

—Open it an' see, son.

Darren did.

—It's a pump.

—That's righ', said Jimmy Sr. —It's a good one too.

Darren didn't understand. He looked at his da's face.

—I'll get yeh a wheel for your Christmas, said Jimmy Sr. —An' the other one for your next birthd'y. An' then the

97

saddle. An' before yeh know it you'll have your bike. How's tha'?

Darren looked at the pump, then at his da. His da was smiling but it wasn't a joking smile. He looked at his ma. She had her back to him, at the sink. Now he understood. He understood now: he'd just been given a poxy pump for his birthday. And he was going to be getting bits of bike for the rest of his life and ——But the twins were giggling. And now so was Sharon.

His brother, Jimmy, stood up and was putting on his jacket.

—Yeh can pump yourself to school every mornin' now, he said.

—Yis are messin', said Darren.

He laughed. He knew it. He had a bike. He knew it.

—Yis are messin'!

Jimmy Sr laughed.

—We are o' course.

He opened the back door and went out, and came back in with a bike, a big old black grocer's delivery bike with a frame over the front wheel but no basket in it.

—Get up on tha' now an' we'll see how it fits, said Jimmy Sr.

—Wha'? said Darren.

His mouth was wide open. Veronica was laughing now.

—It's a Stephen Roche special, said Jimmy Sr.

Darren was still staring at the bike. Then he noticed the others laughing.

He looked around at them.

—Yis are messin'.

He laughed, louder now than before.

—Yis are still messin'.

—We are o' course, said Jimmy Sr.

He patted the saddle.

—This is Bimbo's.

He wheeled it out, and wheeled in the real present. Larrygogan followed it in.

—Ah rapid! Da ——Ma —.Thanks. Rapid. Ah deadly.

He held the bike carefully.

—A Raleigh! Deadly. ——Ten gears! Great. Muggah's only got five.

Jimmy Sr laughed.

—Only the best, he said.

—Raleighs aren't the best, Darren told him. —Peugeots and Widersprints are.

He was looking at his new bike and adoring it; its thinness, neatness, shininess, the colour, the pedals with the straps on them and, most of all, the handlebars.

—Yeh ungrateful little bollix, said Jimmy Sr. —Give us tha' back.

He grabbed the bike and pushed Darren away from it.

Darren was lost. He didn't know what he'd done. He didn't know. His eyes filled. He just stood there.

Jimmy Sr pushed the bike back to him.

—There.

——Thanks, Da. Thanks, Ma.

—Mammy.

—Mammy. It's brilliant.

He wolfed his breakfast, then cycled across the road to school.

* * *

It was about six o'clock the same day, Jimmy Sr, washed and ready, sat down at the kitchen table. But the dinner wasn't ready.

—How come? he wanted to know.

—I started on the girls' dresses, said Veronica.

—Wha' dresses?

—Ballroom.

—Jaysis.

—Stop that. ——Anyway, I forgot the time.

Jimmy Sr was in good form.

—Ah well, he said. —Not to worry. I'll have a slice o' bread. That'll keep me goin'.

He didn't bother with the marge.

—How ——are yeh today, Veronica? he asked.

—Okay. Grand. I'm tired now though.

—Cummins said he might have somethin' for Leslie in a few weeks.

—I'll believe it when I see it, said Veronica.

—I suppose so, said Jimmy Sr. —He said he'll ask round an' see if anny of his pals have annythin' for him. Yeh know, the golf an' church collection shower.

—You wouldn't want to be relying on them.

—True.

He began to demolish another couple of slices.

—Still ——what else can we do? ——I had five fuckin' jobs to choose from when I got thrun out o' school. Where is he?

—Who?

—Leslie.

—I don't know. Out.

—I haven't seen him in ages. Weeks —Yeah, weeks. Wha' does he look like?

Veronica laughed.

—He's not hangin' round the house annyway, said Jimmy Sr. —Gettin' under your feet.

—No.

—That's somethin'. But he should have his breakfasts an' his dinners with the rest of us. The family tha' eats together ——How does it go?

Veronica was prodding the potatoes.

Darren came in, on his way out. He was wearing a Carrera cycling jersey Jimmy Jr had just given him. It nearly reached his knees. He was trying to rub the creases out of it. When he looked down the zip touched his nose.

—That's a great yoke, Darren, Jimmy Sr told him —It'll fit yeh properly in a couple o' months, wha'.

—It'll be too small, said Veronica, —the way he's growing. Where d'you think you're going to?

—Ou', said Darren.

—Not till after your tea you're not, said Veronica.

—Ah Ma. Round the block only?

—Let him go, said Jimmy Sr. —He wants to show off his jersey to the young ones.

Darren was out the door.

Jimmy Jr came into the kitchen.

—Was tha' jersey yoke dear? Jimmy Sr asked him.

Jimmy Jr tapped the side of his nose with a finger, and winked. Jimmy Sr raised his eyebrows. He looked at Veronica. She was turning the chops.

—Did no one actually buy the poor fucker a present? he whispered.

Jimmy Jr grinned, and went upstairs to change.

Sharon came in from work.

—There's Sharon, said Jimmy Sr. —How are yeh, Sharon?

—Grand.

—Good. That's the way to be. Your face is nice an' pink.

—Thanks very much!

—Very healthy lookin'. Is he kickin'?

—He's doin' cartwheels.

—We'll have to get him a bike like Darren's so.

Sharon sat down.

—That's righ', Sharon, said Jimmy Sr. —Sit down.

The twins were in the hall.

They heard Linda.

—Slow – Slow – Quick – Quick – Slow. ——Ah, watch it! You're supposed to be the man, yeh fuckin' eejit.

—Tell them to stop that language, said Veronica.

—Stop tha' language, Jimmy Sr shouted.

—Linda said it, said Tracy from the hall.

—You made me.

—I didn't.

—Did. ——Come on. Your fingers are supposed to be at righ' angles to my spine. ——Slow – Slow – Quick – Quick – Slow.

—What's goin' on ou' there? said Jimmy Sr.

He leaned back so he could see out into the hall. He grinned as he watched Linda and Tracy going through their steps. They hit the stairs.

—You're doin' it wrong, he said. —Look.

He got up and went into the hall.

Sharon grinned.

Veronica was dividing the food onto the plates.

—D'yeh need a hand, Mammy? said Sharon.

—No.

They heard Jimmy Sr.

—Now. Are yis watchin'? Yeh put your feet slightly apart, d'yeh see? Like this. ——Now, I put my weight on me left foot. An' wha' foot do you put your weight on?

—The righ' one, said Linda.

—Good girl, said Jimmy Sr. —Cos you're the lady. ——Then, look it, I side-step like tha' —an' we're off. Step – Step – Cha Cha Cha – Step – Step – Cha Cha Cha —

Sharon laughed.

—I didn't know Daddy could dance like tha', she said.

—Neither did I, said Veronica. —Now, where is everyone? Why do they all disappear just when their dinner's ready?

They heard Jimmy Sr.

—Step – Step – Cha Cha Cha —An' there we go. Your turn, Tracy. ——No, wrong foot. You're the lady. Good girl. An' off we go. Two – Three – Four —an' One – Two

– Three – Four —an' One – Step – Step – Cha Cha Cha. It's all comin' back to me.

—Dinner, Veronica roared.

Jimmy Jr came in.

—Has Da been drinkin'?

Jimmy Sr was in after him, followed by Linda and Tracy.

—Do we still have tha' Joe Loss LP, Veronica? ——Wha' are you grinnin' at?

He was talking to Jimmy Jr.

—LP, Jimmy Jr sneered. —It's an album.

—Oh, said Jimmy Sr. —I forgot. We've Larry fuckin' Gogan here with us for the dinner. Spinnin' the discs, wha'. ——It's an LP, righ'.

—Fair enough, Twinkletoes.

—I'll fuckin' —

—Shut up and eat your dinner, said Veronica.

—Certainly, Veronica, said Jimmy Sr.

He looked down at his dinner.

—My God now, tha' looks lovely. I'm starvin' after all tha' dancin'. I could eat the left leg o' the Lamb o' ——

—Don't! said Veronica.

Jimmy Sr chewed, and swallowed.

—Mind you, girls, he told the twins. —I always preferred the Cucarachas to the Cha Cha Cha. You can really swing your lady in the Cucarachas.

Jimmy Jr laughed. So did Sharon.

—Fuck yis, said Jimmy Sr.

Darren dashed in. He had news for them.

—Pat said his da's after runnin' away from home.

Jimmy Sr looked up from his dinner.

—Pat who?

—Burgess.

Jimmy Sr burst out laughing. Jimmy Jr and the others joined in.

—Is Georgie Burgess after runnin' away? said Jimmy Sr.

—Yeah, said Darren. —Pat said he fucked —ran off last nigh'. His ma's up to ninety. He's says she's knockin' back the Valiums like there's no tomorrow.

—She would, said Veronica.

—Poor Doris, said Jimmy Sr. —That's a good one though.

—Here, said Jimmy Jr. —He's prob'ly gone off to join the French Foreign Legion.

—That's righ', yeah. Where's he gone, Darren?

—Don't know. Pat doesn't know. He said he just snuck ou'.

—Sneaked, said Veronica.

—Yeah, righ'.

—That's a good one all the same.

Jimmy Sr was delighted.

—Where's Sharon gone?

—She must be gone to the jacks.

—She's always in there.

—Leave her alone. She can't help it, said Jimmy Sr. ——Ran away, wha'. ——That's a lovely chop.

—That's a lovely chop, said Linda.

—Don't start, you, said Jimmy Sr.

He grinned.

—Who'll be managin' yis now, Darren?

—Don't know, said Darren. —He might come back.

—Jaysis, I hope not.

Jimmy Sr filled his mouth again.

——Ran away, wha'.

—Yeah, said Jr.

—Tom Sawyer, said Jimmy Sr.

He laughed.

* * *

Sharon was in her parents' bedroom, looking out across at the Burgess's.

It was frightening. She was sure Mister Burgess running away had something to do with her but she hadn't a clue what. And she was sure as well that this wasn't the end of it; there was more to come.

What though? She didn't know. Something terrible, something really terrible ——

Oh God ——

She'd have to wait and see.

She stood up off the bed. The bad shakes were gone. Her chest didn't hurt as much. She'd go down and finish her dinner.

On the way down she went into the toilet and flushed it.

* * *

—Tom Sawyer, wha', said Jimmy Sr.

—Exactly, said Bimbo.

They all laughed again.

—That's the best ever, said Bimbo. —Gas.

—He must have a mot hidden away somewhere, said Paddy.

—Si, Bertie agreed.

—Who'd fuckin' look at HIM? Jimmy Sr wanted to know. —The state of him.

—Have yeh looked at yourself recently? Paddy asked him.

—I'm not runnin' away, am I? said Jimmy Sr. —Fuckin' off an' —an' shirkin' my responsibilities.

—Shirkin'? said Bertie.

—Fuck off.

—He's not tha' bad, said Bimbo.

—Yeh fancy him yourself, do yeh?

—No!

Bertie and Paddy laughed.

—Bimbo goes for the younger lads, Jimmy Sr told them.
—Isn't tha' righ'?

—Ah lay off, will yeh. ——I can't understand it. Yeh know, the way queers —like each other.

—D'yeh think about it much? Paddy asked him.

—No! ——Nearly never. Lay off.

Bertie put his pint down.

—So the Signor Burgess has vamoosed, he said.

—An' shirked his responsibilities, said Paddy.

—Fuck off, you, said Jimmy Sr.

—Poor Doris an' the kids, said Bimbo.

—Why don't you adopt them? said Paddy.

—Would you ever leave me alone, said Bimbo.

—Tell him to fuck off, said Jimmy Sr.

—I will, said Bimbo. —Fuck off.

—Make me.

* * *

What WAS he up to anyway?

Sharon pulled on her other boot. She sat up slowly. God Jesus, her back really hurt her when she did that, after being bent down. She put her hands on her belly. She could feel it shifting.

What was he fuckin' up to?

The baby butted her.

—Take it easy, will yeh, said Sharon.

She got her money off the bed and put it in her bag. She hoped to God Yvonne wouldn't be there tonight. Maybe she'd be better off staying at home ——

—Ah fuck this, she said.

And she got up and went out.

* * *

—Jesus; poor Yvonne though, said Jackie.

—Yeah, said Mary and Sharon.

—Maybe we should go round to her, said Jackie.

—Ah no, said Sharon.

—Yeah, said Mary. —I'd be too embarrassed.

—Mm, said Jackie. —Can yeh imagine it? Jesus!

—Jesus, yeah.

* * *

She waited. She knew she'd have to get up and go to the toilet at least once more.

He was going to do something really stupid, she was certain of that.

She sat up. She'd go to the toilet now.

Something really, really stupid.

She'd just have to wait and see, that was all. ——People were going to find out ——her mammy and daddy ——! Oh God, if that —!

She'd just have to wait and see.

She got back into bed.

* * *

Sharon wasn't long waiting and seeing. Linda woke her up. This was the night after Darren had broken the big news.

—Sharon, said Linda.

She was scared.

—There's someone throwin' things at the window.

—Yeah, said Tracy.

She wouldn't get out of the bed.

—Who's throwin' things? said Sharon.

—Don't know.

—Yeah.

—Let's see, said Sharon.

—I'm not lookin', said Linda.

Sharon went over to the window. Just before she reached it there was a neat little bang.

—Oh janey! said one of the twins.

Someone had flung something at it. That frightened Sharon. She parted the curtain a little bit. The bedroom light was out but she could see nothing in the garden.

But then she saw someone, behind the hedge at the back, in the field. He —it looked like a man —was bent down. Then he stood up and came through the gap in the hedge, over the wire, and it was Mister Burgess.

Sharon nearly died.

He stood there in the middle of the garden at the place where Les was supposed to do the digging. He was looking up at her window. —How did he know? —Then she saw his hand move up from his side, the palm towards her. Then there was another bang.

She jumped. He'd just lobbed a little stone at the window. She let go of the curtain.

—Who is it, Sharon?

—Just young fellas, said Sharon. —Messin'.

—Messin'! said Tracy. —At this hour o' night.

—I'll get them tomorrow, said Sharon.

—Wha' young fellas? said Linda.

Sharon parted the curtain again. Mister Burgess wasn't there. She didn't think he was behind the hedge or the trees in the field either.

—They're gone now, she said.

—Let's see, said Linda.

She looked.

—They're gone, Tracy, she said.

—Night nigh', said Sharon.

She was back in bed.

—Nigh' nigh', said Linda.

Tracy was sleeping.

Was Mister Burgess getting all romantic on her? Sharon wondered. Jesus, that was disgusting. Maybe he'd gone weird, like one of those men on the News ——

She'd have to wait and see a bit more.

She lay there, wide awake.

* * *

Jimmy Sr turned the sound down a bit.

—I'll never lay a hand on the twins again, he told Sharon.

—Wha'?

—The twins, said Jimmy Sr. —I'll never touch them again.

—Did you hit them?

—No! ——No; it's all tha' child abuse stuff goin' on over in England. Were yeh not watchin' it?

—No. I was miles away.

—On the News there, Jimmy Sr explained. —It looks like yeh can't look at your own kids over there. They'll take them away from yeh. An' inspect their arses —

—Daddy!

—It's true, Jimmy Sr insisted.

They were by themselves in the front room.

—Half the fuckin' doctors in England are spendin' their time lookin' up children's holes.

—You're disgustin'.

—It's not me, Sharon, said Jimmy Sr. —Yeh can't turn on the fuckin' telly or open a paper or ——there's somethin' abou' child abuse. The kids must be scared stiff.

—But it happens, said Sharon.

—Maybe it does, I don't know. I suppose it does. ——I'd kill annyone tha' did somethin' like tha' to a child. A little kid. They do it to snappers even. I'd chop his bollix —excuse me, Sharon —off. I would. Then hang him. Or shoot him. ——At least it's not goin' on over here.

—You'd never know, said Sharon.

—Would yeh say so? said Jimmy Sr. —Maybe you're righ'. Jaysis. ——It's shockin'. How could annyone —

Darren came in.

—Good man, Darren, said Jimmy Sr. —Have yeh come in for your cyclin'?

—Yeah, said Darren.

He sat down on the floor.

—Channel 4, said Jimmy Sr. —Let's see now.

He studied the remote control.

—Number one.

He pressed it.

—Ads, he said. —That's it. How's Kelly doin', Darren?

—Alrigh'.

——He's gettin' old, said Jimmy Sr. —The oul' legs. Wha' abou' Roche?

—Fourth.

—He hasn't a hope, said Jimmy Sr.

—He has so.

—Not at all, said Jimmy Sr. —He's too nice, that's his problem. He doesn't have the killer instinct.

—He won the Giro, Darren reminded him.

—Fluke, said Jimmy Sr. —Hang on, here it is.

He turned up the sound.

—The music's great, isn't it?

—Yeah, said Darren and Sharon.

—Good Jaysis, said Jimmy Sr. —Look at those mountains. Roche is fucked. There's no mountains like tha' in Ireland.

—Ah shut up, Da, will yeh.

—I'm only expressin' me opinion.

—Yeh haven't a clue.

Jimmy Sr nudged Sharon. Then he switched channels.

—Aaah!

—Sorry. Sorry, Darren. Me finger slipped, sorry

——There; that's it back. There's Roche now. He's strugglin', look it. I told yeh. He's not smilin' now, wha'.

—Da!

Jimmy Sr grinned and nudged Sharon again.

* * *

Sharon got home from work a bit early on Monday, five days after she'd seen Mister Burgess throwing stones at the window. She hadn't been feeling well, like as if she'd eaten too much chocolate, and the bottom of her back was killing her.

She took a box of cod steaks from her bag.

—I got these out o' work, she told her mother.

—You'll get caught, said Veronica.

—No, I won't, said Sharon.

—It's not right. There's a letter over there for you.

—For me?

The envelope was white and the address was in ordinary writing. Sharon had never got a real letter before.

—That's a man's writing, said Veronica.

Sharon looked at her.

—I didn't open it.

—I never thought yeh did, Mammy, said Sharon.

But she went upstairs to read it. Linda and Tracy were down watching the telly or practising their dancing. Something had been written on the back of the envelope but it had been rubbed over with the same pen. She couldn't make it out. She opened the envelope carefully, afraid she'd rip what was inside. She gasped, then groaned, —Oh my God, and sat down on her bed when she saw what the letter was about. She should have guessed it, but she hadn't; not really.

There was no address or date.

Dear Sharon,

I hope you are well. Please meet me in the Abbey Mooney in town at 8 o'clock on Tuesday night. I want to talk to you about something very important. I am looking forward to seeing you.

Yours sincerely
George Burgess.

There was a P.S.

The paper is my sisters.

The writing paper was pink. There was a bunny rabbit in the top left corner, sitting in some light blue and yellow flowers.

Sharon sat there. She just sat there.

Then she sort of shook herself, and realized that she was angry.

The fucker.

There was no way she was going to meet him, no fuckin' way. She lifted the flap of the envelope up to the light coming through the window. She could make out the shapes of the rubbed-out writing on the flap now. They were capital letters.

S.W.A.L.K.

—Oh, the fuckin' eejit! said Sharon.

*   *   *

Bertie came in.

—There y'are, Bertie, said Bimbo.

—Howyeh, Bertie.

—Buenas noches, compadres, said Bertie.

—It's your round, Paddy told him.

—Give us a chance, for the sake of fuck.

As Bertie said this he sat down and lifted his hand, showing four fingers to Leo the barman.

—How's the Jobsearch goin', Bertie? Jimmy Sr asked him.

—Don't talk to me abou' Jobsearch.

He pretended to spit on the ground.

—I speet on Jobsearch.

Bimbo and Jimmy Sr laughed and Paddy grinned.

—D'yis know wha' they had me doin' today, do yis? Yis won't believe this.

—Wha'? said Bimbo.

—They were teachin' us how to use the phone.

—Wha'!?

—I swear to God. The fuckin' phone.

—You're not serious.

—I am, yeh know. I fuckin' am. The gringo in charge handed ou' photocopies of a diagram of a phone. I think I have it ——No, I left it back at the Ponderosa. I'll show it to yis tomorrow. ——A fuckin' phone.

—Don't listen to him.

—It's true, I'm tellin' yeh. I was embarrassed for him, the poor cunt. He knew it was fuckin' stupid himself. You could tell; the poor fucker tellin' us where to put the tenpences. One chap told him where he could stick the tenpences an' then he walked ou'.

They laughed.

—Then he was tellin' us, Bertie continued, —wha' we should an' shouldn't say when we're lookin' for work.

—Wha' should yeh not say? Bimbo asked.

—Anny chance of a fuckin' job there, pal.

They laughed.

—It was the greatest waste o' fuckin' time, said Bertie. —You should always tell the name o' the paper yeh saw the ad in. There now. An' there's no job ads in the Mirror.

Unless it's the manager o' Spurs or Man United or some-thin'. ——I wouldn't mind, compadres, but I've abou' thirty fuckin' phones in cold storage. Mickey Mouse an' Snoopy ones.

—Jessica'd like a Snoopy one, said Bimbo. —For her birth'y.

—You don't have a phone, said Paddy.

—So?

—So a Snoopy one won't be much use to Jessica, will it?

—For an ornament, I meant. For her bedside locker.

—Her wha'?

—Her bedside locker.

—I bet yeh you made it yourself.

—No! ——I bought it an' put it together.

Paddy raised his eyes to heaven.

—Do anny of yis ever hit your kids? Jimmy Sr asked them all.

He lowered a third of his latest pint while they looked at him.

—Never, said Bimbo.

—Now an' again, said Paddy.

—Well, yeah, said Bimbo. —Now an' again, alrigh'. When they're lookin' for it. Specially Wayne.

—It's the only exercise I get, Bertie told them. —I wait till they're old enough to run but. To give them a fair chance, yeh know.

Bimbo knew he was joking, so he laughed.

—I'm dyin' to give Gillian a good hidin', said Bertie. —But she never does annythin' bold. She'd give yeh the sick. Trevor's great though. Trevor's a desperado.

Jimmy Sr took control of the conversation again.

—Yis'd want to be careful, he told them.

—Why's tha', compadre?

—Cos if you're caught you're fucked.

—What're yeh on abou'? said Paddy.

—Child abuse, said Jimmy Sr.

—Would yeh ever fuck off, said Paddy. —Givin' your kids a smack for bein' bold isn't child abuse.

—No way.

—I don't know, said Jimmy Sr. —It looks to me like yeh can't look crooked at your kids now —

—Don't be thick, said Paddy. —You're exaggeratin'. Yeh have to burn them with cigarette butts or —

—I'm not listenin' to this, said Bimbo.

—Don't then, said Paddy. —Or mess around with their —

—SHUT UP.

It was Bimbo. Paddy stopped.

—You're makin' a joke of it, said Bimbo.

—I'm not.

—Yeh are.

—Whose twist is it? said Bertie. —Someone's shy.

—Four pints, Leo, Jimmy Sr shouted. —Like a good man. ——Maybe you're righ', he said to both Bimbo and Paddy. —It's shockin' though, isn't it? The whole business.

—Fuckin' terrible, said Bimbo.

—Come here, said Bertie. —Guess who I spied with my little eye this mornin'.

—Who?

—Someone beginnin' with B.

—Burgess!

—Si.

—Great. Where?

—Swords.

—How was he lookin'? said Jimmy Sr.

—Oh, very thin an' undernourished, said Bertie. —An' creased.

—Yahaah!

Jimmy Sr rubbed his hands.

—I nearly gave the poor cunt twopence, Bertie told them.

They liked that.

—There mustn't be another mot so, said Paddy. —If he's in rag order like tha'.

—Unless she's a brasser.

—Were yeh talkin' to him? Bimbo asked.

—No, said Bertie. —I was on me way to learn how to use the phone.

—Now, Leo called. —Four nice pints over here.

—Leo wants yeh, Paddy told Jimmy Sr.

Jimmy Sr brought the pints down to the table and sat down. Bertie picked up the remains of his old pint.

—To the Signor Horge Burgess, he said.

—Oh def'ny, said Bimbo.

They raised their glasses.

—The fuckin' eejit, said Jimmy Sr.

—Ah now, said Bertie. —That's not nice.

*   *   *

Sharon was nowhere near the Abbey Mooney at eight o'clock on Tuesday.

She lay in bed later, half expecting stones to start hitting the window. Or something.

*   *   *

It was that Sharon Rabbitte one from across the road. She was pregnant. She'd come to the house. She was the one; she knew it.

Dear Doris,
     I hope you are well——

People probably knew already. They always did around here. Oh God, the shame; the mortification. She'd never be able to step out of the house again.

I am writing to you to let you know why I left you last week —

If he'd died and left her a widow it would've been different, alright; but this wasn't fair. He was making her feel ashamed, the selfish bastard, and she hadn't done anything.

Doris, I've been having a bit of an affair with a girl. This girl is expecting —

The Rabbitte one; it had to be.

I am very sorry —

It had to be.

I hope you will understand, Doris. I cannot abandon this girl. She has no one else to look after her —

The next bit was worse.

I still love you, Doris. But I love this girl as well. I am, as the old song goes, torn between two lovers. I will miss you and the children very much —

Oh God!
He was her husband!
Twenty-four years. It wasn't her fault.

P.S.
I got a lend of the paper.

Doris sniffed.
He'd always been an eejit. She'd never be able to go out

again. ——Men got funny at George's age. She'd noticed the same thing with her father. They went silly when there were girls near them; when her friends had been in the house. They tried to pretend that they weren't getting old and made eejits out of themselves. And, God knew, George had a head start there.

The Rabbitte one probably took money off him as well.

* * *

Veronica made out Doris Burgess's shape through the glass. The hair was the give-away.

She opened the door.

—Doris, she said.

—Is Sharon in? said Doris.

—She's at work. Why?

Veronica knew; before she had it properly worked out.

Doris tried to look past Veronica.

—Why do you want her? said Veronica.

Now Doris looked at Veronica.

—Well, if you must know, she's been messin' around with George. ——He's the father.

—Get lost, Doris, said Veronica.

—I will not get lost now, said Doris. —She's your daughter, isn't she?

There were two women coming up the road, four gates away.

—Of course, said Doris, —what else would you expect from a —

Veronica punched her in the face.

* * *

—What happened yeh, Doris? said Mrs Foster.

—Tha' one hit her, said Mrs Caprani. —Yeh seen it yourself.

—I mean before that.

Doris wanted to get out of Rabbitte territory. She pulled herself away from the women and ran out the gate. She stopped on the path.

—What happened, Doris? Mrs Foster asked again.

She tried to get to Doris's nose with a paper hankie.

More people were coming.

—Veronica Rabbitte's after givin' poor Doris an awful clatter, Mrs Caprani told them. —In the nose.

Doris was still crying.

—I'll do it —it myself.

She took the hankie.

—Wha' happened yeh, Doris?

——Sh —Shar —

—Shar, Doris? What shar?

* * *

Inside, Veronica sat in the kitchen, putting sequins onto Linda's dancing dress.

* * *

Sharon lay on her bed. She couldn't go downstairs, she couldn't go to the Hikers, or anywhere. She was surrounded. She was snared. If she went anywhere or ——she couldn't. All because of that stupid fucker.

—The fucker, she said to the ceiling.

The baby was nothing. It happened. It was alright. Barrytown was good that way. Nobody minded. Guess the daddy was a hobby. But now Burgess —He'd cut her off from everything. She'd no friends now, and no places to go to. She couldn't even look at her family. God, she wanted to die; really she did. She just lay there. She couldn't do anything else.

She was angry now. She thumped the bed.

The bastard, the fucker; it wasn't fuckin' fair. She'd deny it, that was what she'd do. And she'd keep denying it. And denying it.

*　*　*

Veronica and Jimmy Sr were down in the kitchen.

—Desperate, so it is, said Jimmy Sr quietly. —Shockin'.

Veronica put the dress down. She couldn't look at another sequin.

—That's about the hundredth time you've said that, she told him.

—Well, it is fuckin' desperate.

They heard Linda and Tracy coming up the hall.

—Slow – Slow – Quick – Quick ——Slow.

——Get ou'! Jimmy Sr roared.

—We know where we're not wanted, said Linda. —Come on, Tracy.

—Slow – Slow – Quick —

They danced down the hall, into the front room to annoy Darren.

Jimmy Sr was miserable.

—Poor Sharon though.

——Poor Sharon! said Veronica. —What about poor us?

—Don't start now, said Jimmy Sr.

He was playing with a cold chip.

—I suppose ——She could've been more careful, he said.

—She could've had more taste, said Veronica.

—That's righ', said Jimmy Sr, glad to be able to say it. —You're right o' course. That's what's so terrible about it. George Burgess. ——Georgie Burgess. Jesus, Veronica, I think the cunt's older than I am.

He threw the chip at the window, and then felt stupid.

He was feeling sorry for himself; he knew it. And now he was letting his eyes water.

—It's only yourself you're worried about, Veronica told him.

—Ah ——I know, said Jimmy Sr. —But poor Sharon as well.

He rubbed his eyes quickly.

—I can't even go ou' for a fuckin' pint.

—It's about time you stayed in.

—Is there annythin' good on?

—I don't know.

——George fuckin' Burgess.

Then they heard the voice from upstairs.

—THIS IS JIMMY RABBITTE – ALL – OVER – IRELAND.

—Oh fuck, no, Jimmy Sr pleaded. —Not tonigh'. Please.

*   *   *

Jimmy Sr gave Sharon a lift to work the next morning. They didn't say much. Jimmy Sr asked a question.

—How —?

— It wasn't him.

—I never —

—It wasn't him, righ'.

—Okay. ——Okay.

That was it.

*   *   *

Jimmy Sr scooped out the teabag and flung it into a corner. His shoulders were at him. He felt shite. He wanted to go home.

It wasn't him, she'd said.

He didn't know. He tried it again: it wasn't him. He believed her of course, but ——If it wasn't Burgess then who the fuck was it? She'd have to tell them. He had to know for certain that it was definitely someone else; anyone. She'd just have to fuckin' tell them.

Or else.

He tried the tea. It was brutal.

* * *

—There's no fuckin' way, Jackie. You know tha'.

Jackie was sitting on the twins' bed. Sharon was sitting on her own bed. She looked at the steam rising up off her tea, so she didn't have to look at Jackie.

—I know, said Jackie.

It wasn't enough, Jackie knew; not nearly. It didn't sound as if she'd meant it enough.

—I know tha', she said; better this time, she thought.

—Jesus, the state of him. There's no way you'd've —

—Don't say it, said Sharon. —I'll get sick, I swear.

Jackie tried to laugh. They looked at each other and then they really laughed. Sharon thought the happiness would burst out of her, through her ribs, out of her mouth.

—Can yeh imagine it! she said.

—Tha' dirty big belly on top o' yeh!

—Stop it!

They said nothing for a bit, and the giggling died. Sharon's nails dug into her palms.

—I KNOW WHA' YOU'RE THIN —KIN', she sang.

Jackie laughed, at the floor.

—Fuck off, she said. ——Are yeh tellin'?

—S'pose I'd better.

——Jesus, Sharon, come on.

—It was one o' them Spanish sailors.

—Wha'?

—Yeh know, said Sharon. —Yeh do. In the Harp, I met him.

—Oh, now I get yeh. Jesus, Sharon.

—There was loads o' them there, yeh know. There was a big boat, yeh know; down in the docks for two days, I think it was.

She had this bit off by heart.

—He was gorgeous, Jackie, I'm not jokin' yeh.

—Was he? Jesus. ——Yeh never mentioned him before.

—No. I didn't want to. ——Yeh know. It was only for one night.

—Yeah. Do yeh know his address?

—I don't even know his fuckin' name, Jackie.

Manuel was the only Spanish name she could think of.

—Jesus, said Jackie. —Go on annyway.

—Ah, I just met him. In the Harp, yeh know. His English was brutal. ——Come here, he had a sword.

She'd just thought up that bit.

—I'd say he did alrigh', said Jackie, and they roared laughing.

—That's disgustin', Jackie.

—Where did yis —do it? Jackie asked.

She was smiling. She was enjoying herself now.

—In his hotel. The Ormond, yeh know.

—Was he not supposed to sleep in his ship?

—No, not really. They let them ou' for the night.

—Oh yeah. ——Like Letter To Brezhnev.

—God, yeah, said Sharon. —Jesus, I never thought o' tha'.

She was sure her nails had gone through the skin.

—Was he nice?

—Fuckin' gorgeous. Anyway, I wouldn't've done it with him if he hadn't o' been, sure I wouldn't?

—No way.

—He was very dark.

She hoped to God the baby wouldn't have red hair.

—Was he good?

—Fuckin' brilliant. He had me nearly screamin', I'm not jokin' yeh.

—Oh —

—We did it in the bath as well.

—God, I'd love tha'.

—It was brilliant.

—Yeah, said Jackie. —Yeh lucky bitch yeh, Sharon. I'm goin' to go to the Harp from now on. ——Come here, did he give you his cap?

—Wha'?

—His cap. Yeh know. His uniform.

—Ah, no.

—Did he not? ——Yeh know Melanie Beglin? She has two o' them. A German an' a Swedish.

—Does she?

—Yeah. She's a slut, tha' one. ——Jesus, sorry, Sharon! I didn't mean —

Sharon laughed.

—She is though, said Jackie. —I hate her. Come here, Sharon, though. Why did Mister Burgess run away?

—I don't know!

—I know it wasn't ——because. Yeh know. But —Let's go an' get pissed.

—Ah —

—Go on, Sharon. Howth. A bit o' buzz.

—Okay. Where's me shoes?

—There, look it. I'll get them.

—No, it's alrigh'. Jesus, me fuckin' back. ——How's Yvonne takin' it?

——

—Will yeh tell her about the sailor? said Sharon.

—Okay.

—Thanks.

* * *

—I'll be blinded by these bloody sequins, said Veronica.

—Wha'? said Jimmy Sr.

—Look it, said Veronica. —I'm still on Linda's one.

She held up the dress.

—It looks like I've only started.

——That's shockin', said Jimmy Sr. —Why couldn't they just play basketball or somethin'? It looks very nice though, Veronica.

—Mm.

Jimmy Sr wriggled around on the couch. It was past his going out time.

—D'yeh know wha', Veronica? I'm nearly afraid to go down to the pub ——because of —

—Oh, shut up.

——Do you believe her, Veronica?

—Shut up.

* * *

There was a bunch of kids, boys Darren's age, sitting on the wall at the bus-stop when Sharon got off. They all stared at her as she went past them. When she'd gone about three gates one of them shouted.

—How's Mister Burgess?

She didn't turn or stop.

—Yeh ride yeh.

She kept walking.

They were only kids.

Still, she was shaking and kind of upset when she got home and upstairs. She didn't know why really. Men and boys had been shouting things after her since she was thirteen and fourteen. She'd never liked it much, especially when she was very young, but she'd looked on it as a sort of a stupid compliment.

Tonight was different though. Being called a ride wasn't any sort of a compliment anymore.

*　*　*

—What're YOU fuckin' lookin' at? Jimmy Sr asked Paddy.
He was serious.
—Nothin'.
—D'yeh think I have fuckin' cancer or somethin'?
—No!
—Ah lads, now, said Bimbo. —There's no need for tha' sort o' shite.
—I didn't do annythin', Paddy insisted.
—You were starin' at me, said Jimmy Sr. —Annyway, he said out of nowhere. (They'd been talking about Stephen Roche.) —It wasn't Burgess. It was a Spanish sailor.

*　*　*

—She thinks he was Spanish annyway, Jackie told Mary.
—Where? said Mary.
—The Harp.
—Oh, yeah. ——D'you believe her?
——Yeah. It couldn't have been —
—No.
—Will Yvonne believe it, d'yeh think? Jackie asked.
—Emm ——she might.
—She won't, sure she won't?
—No. ——She might though.

*　*　*

Two nights after Sharon told Jackie about the Spanish sailor George Burgess was waiting for her outside work.

—God! said Sharon. —How did you know where I worked?

—Did yeh not see me at the vegetables?

He was having problems holding up his smile.

—What d'you want, Mister Burgess?

—George.

—Mister Burgess.

—Yeh didn't turn up on Tuesday.

—I know I didn't. Wha' d'yeh want?

—I want to talk to yeh, Sharon.

—That's a pity now, Mister Burgess, cos I don't want to talk to you.

—Ah Sharon, please. I have to talk.

The smile was gone.

—I'm tormented.

—You're tormented! Yeh prick yeh. Who's been flingin' rocks at my window? An' how did yeh know it was my window annyway? An' sendin' me stupid fuckin' letters. Well? ——You've made me the laughin' stock o' Barry-town, that I can't even go ou' without bein' jeered. You're tormented! Fuck off, Mister Burgess.

She started to walk around him. He was going to stop her, but then he didn't. He walked with her.

—Look, Sharon, I swear I'll leave you alone. On the Bible; forever. If yeh just listen to me for a minute. I swear.

—Fuck off.

—Please, Sharon. Please.

—Get your fuckin' hands off me!

But she stopped.

—Wha'? she said.

—Here?

—Yeah.

—Can we not go into a pub or —or a coffee place or somethin'?

—No, we can't. Come on, I'm in a hurry.

—Okay.

She was watching Mister Burgess blushing.

—Sharon, he said. —Sharon ——I love you, Sharon. Don't laugh; I do! I swear. On the —— I love you. I'm very embarrassed, Sharon. I've been thinkin' about it. ——I think I —I want to take care of you —

—You took care of me five months ago. Goodbye, Mister Burgess.

She walked on.

—It's my son too, remember, said George.

—Son!?

—Baby, I meant baby.

—Your baby?

She couldn't stop the laugh coming out.

—You've got it bad, haven't you, Mister Burgess?

—I have, Sharon; yeah.

He sighed. He looked at the ground. Then he looked at her for a second.

— I've always liked yeh, Sharon; you know tha'. I ——Sharon, I've been livin' a lie for the last fifteen years. Twenty years. The happily married man. Huh. It's taken you to make me cop on. You, Sharon.

—Did you rehearse this, Mister Burgess?

—No. ——Yeah, I did. I've thought o' nothin' else, to be honest with yeh. I've been eatin an' drinkin' an' sleepin' —sleepin' it, Sharon.

—Bye bye, Mister Burgess.

—Come to London with me, Sharon.

—Wha'!?

—I've a sister, another one, lives there an' —

—Would you ever —

—Please, Sharon; let me finish. ——Thanks. Avril. Me sister. She lives very near QPR's place, yeh know. Loftus Road. She'd put us up no problem, till we get a place of our own. I'll get a —

—Stop.

Sharon looked straight at him. It wasn't easy.

—I'm not goin' annywhere with yeh, Mister Burgess. I'm stayin' here. An' it's not YOUR baby either. It's not yours or annyone else's. Will yeh leave me alone now?

—Is it because I'm older than yeh?

—It's because I hate the fuckin' sight of yeh.

—Oh. ——You're not just sayin' tha'?

—No. I hate yeh. Will I sing it for yeh?

—What abou' the little baby?

—Look; forget about the little baby, righ'. If yeh must know, you were off-target tha' time annyway.

—I was not!

That was going too far.

—Yeh were. So now.

Then she remembered.

—An' anyway, it was a Spanish sailor, if yeh must know.

——Spanish?

—Yeah. I sleep around, Mister Burgess. D'yeh know what I mean?

—I find tha' hard to believe, Sharon.

Sharon laughed.

—Go home, Mister Burgess. George. Go home.

—But —

—If yeh really want to do me a favour —

—Annythin', Sharon. You know I'd —

—Shut up before yeh make an even bigger sap of yourself. Sorry. ——Don't ever talk abou' wha' we did to annyone again; okay?

—Righ', Sharon; okay. It'll be our —

—Bye bye.

She went.

He didn't follow.

—I'll always remember you, Sharon.

Sharon laughed again, quietly. That was that out of the way. She hoped. She felt better now. That poor man was some eejit.

* * *

Sharon grabbed the boy. She held him by the hood of his sweatshirt.

—Let go o' me!

She was twice as big as him. He wriggled and elbowed and tried to pull away from her but he wasn't getting anywhere. They heard cloth ripping.

——You're after ripping me hoodie, said the boy.

He stopped squirming. He was stunned. His ma had only bought it for him last week. When she saw it she'd —

Sharon slapped him across the head.

—Wha'!

—Wha' did yeh call me? said Sharon, and she slapped him again.

—I didn't call yeh ann'thin'!

Sharon held onto the hood and swung him into the wall. There was another rip, a long one.

—If you ever call me annythin' again I'll fuckin' kill yeh, d'yeh hear me?

The boy stood there against the wall, afraid to move in case there was another tear.

—D'yeh hear me?

He said nothing. His mates were at the corner, watching. Sharon looked down quickly to see if there was room. Then she lifted her leg and kneed him.

—There, she said.

She'd never done it before. It was easy. She'd do it again.

For a while the boy forgot about his ripped hoodie and his ma.

Sharon looked back, to make sure that he was still alive. He was. His mates were around him, in stitches.

* * *

—She's a fuckin' lyin' bitch, said Yvonne. —I don't care wha' yeh say.

* * *

Jimmy Sr was in the kitchen. So were Sharon and Veronica. Veronica wished she wasn't.

So did Sharon.

—D'yeh expect us to believe tha'? Jimmy Sr asked her, again. —Yeh met this young fella. Yeh —yeh clicked with him. An' yeh went to a hotel with him an' —an' yeh can't even remember his fuckin' name.

—I was drunk I said, said Sharon.

—I was drunk when I met your mother, said Jimmy Sr. —But I still remember her name. It's Veronica!

—Don't shout, said Veronica.

—Ah look, I was really drunk, said Sharon. —Pissed. Sorry, Mammy.

—How do yeh know he was Spanish then? said Jimmy Sr.

He had her.

—Or a sailor.

He had her alright.

—He could've been a Pakistani postman if you were tha' drunk. ——Well?

Sharon stood up.

—Yis needn't believe me if yeh don't want to.

There wasn't enough room for her to run out so she had to get around Jimmy Sr's chair as quick as she could. Jimmy

Sr turned to watch her but he didn't say anything. He turned back to the table.

—Wha' d'yeh think? he asked Veronica.

Veronica was flattening the gold paper from a Cadbury's Snack —she always had a few of them hidden away from the kids for when she wanted one herself —with a fingernail.

—I think, she said, —I'd be delighted if the father was a Spanish sailor and not George Burgess.

—God, yeah, said Jimmy Sr.

—Why don't you leave her alone then?

—Wha' d'yeh mean, Veronica?

—If she says he was a Spanish sailor why not let her say it?

—An' believe her?

Veronica shrugged.

—Yeah.

—I don't know, said Jimmy Sr. —It'd be great. ——If she'd just give us a name or somethin'.

—Does it matter?

—Wha'? ——Maybe you're righ'.

He stood up.

—Fuck it annyway. ——I'll, eh, give it some thought.

—You do that, said Veronica.

*　*　*

Tracy stayed at the bedroom door. She had something she had to ask Sharon.

She got it out.

—Sharon, sure the baby won't look like Mister Burgess?

—Aaah! No, he won't! He's not the daddy, Tracy; I told yeh.

She eyed Tracy.

—Who said that annyway?

—Nicola 'Malley, said Tracy.

—Well, you tell Nicola 'Malley ——to fuck off.

They grinned.

—I did already, said Tracy.

—Good.

—An' I scraped her face as well.

—Good.

—An' Linda scribbled all over her sums.

Sharon laughed.

—Brilliant.

*　*　*

They were nearly finished talking about Bertie's shirt and tie and jacket and why he was wearing them. He'd done a mock interview that afternoon.

—He said he'd've given me the job if there'd been a real job goin', Bertie told them.

—Did he say yeh did annythin' wrong? Paddy asked him.

—Yes, indeed. He said I'd have to stop scratchin' me bollix all the time.

They laughed, but Jimmy Sr didn't.

—Jimmy, said Bertie. —Compadre mio.

—Wha'?

—I just said somethin' funny. Why didn't yeh laugh?

—Sorry, Bertie. I wasn't listenin'. ——I was just lookin' at the soccer shower over there. I think they were laughin' at me.

—Ah cop on, will yeh, said Paddy.

—No; they were, said Jimmy Sr. —Lookin' over, yeh know, an' laughin'.

—No one's laughin' at yeh, said Bertie.

—Not at all, said Bimbo. —They'd want to try.

—Ah sorry, lads. —— It's just —

—You're alrigh', said Bertie.

Jimmy Sr forced himself to smile. They said nothing for a short while.

—She says that it was a Spanish sailor now, said Jimmy Sr. —Sharon.

—So yeh said.

—Why did Burgess fuck off then? Paddy wanted to know.

His wife at home wanted to know as well. So did Bertie and Bimbo.

—That's it, said Jimmy Sr. —I don't fuckin' know. If I knew tha' I'd be able to ——yeh know?

—He must've had some reason, said Paddy.

—Tha' doesn't mean tha' Sharon was the reason, said Bimbo. —It could've been annythin'. Your mot left you for a bit, remember.

—Tha' was different.

—Annyone'd leave him, said Bertie.

—Fuck off, you, said Paddy.

—The way I see it, said Bimbo, —just cos Georgie Burgess ran away an' said he got some young one pregnant an' Sharon is pregnant, yeh know, tha' doesn't mean it has to be Sharon.

He drank.

—That's wha' I think annyway.

—Si, said Bertie.

—Sharon's a lovely lookin' young one, Bimbo told Jimmy Sr. —She'd have young lads queuein' up for her. Burgess wouldn't get near her. I'd say it was the sailor alrigh'.

—This hombre, he speaks the truth, said Bertie.

—A good lookin' young lad, yeh know, said Bimbo. —A bit different as well, yeh know. Dark an' tall. An' —

—Exotic, said Bertie.

—Exactly, said Bimbo.

—An' a hefty langer on him, said Bertie.

They all laughed, even Jimmy Sr.

134

—Christopher Columbus, said Bertie.

They roared.

—You believe her, don't yeh? said Bimbo.

Jimmy held his glass up to the light so he wouldn't have to look at Bimbo or the other two.

—I'd —, he began.

—Course yeh do, said Bimbo.

—Yeah, said Jimmy Sr. —I suppose I do. I def'ny would if I knew —Veronica says I should believe her whether it's true or not.

—She's righ', said Bimbo.

—Yeah, said Jimmy Sr. —Yeah. Whose round is it?

*   *   *

Sharon wasn't sure, but she thought they'd all swallowed it. It made more sense anyway, the lie; it was more believable. No one would ever have believed that herself and Mister Burgess had —she couldn't think of any proper name for it —except for she was pregnant and Mister Burgess had told Missis Burgess that he'd got a young one pregnant. But everyone would easily believe that she'd got off with a Spanish sailor.

So it made more sense. But she knew this as well: everyone would prefer to believe that she'd got off with Mister Burgess. It was a bigger piece of scandal and better gas. She'd have loved it herself, only she was the poor sap who was pregnant. Yeah definitely, Sharon and Mister Burgess was a much better story than Sharon and the Spanish sailor.

So that was what she was fighting against; Barrytown's sense of humour. She'd keep telling them that it was the Spanish sailor and they'd believe her alright, but every time they thought about Mister Burgess with his trousers down and pulling at her tits and watering at the mouth they'd forget about the Spanish sailor.

She should have given him a name. It was too late now. Anyway, her daddy would have been down to the Spanish embassy looking for his address then.

She hated this time of the day, when there weren't enough customers and some of the girls on the check-out had to do the shelves. She was straightening the ranks of shampoo and then she was going to do the same with the soap so she wouldn't have to bend down too much because they were on the middle and top shelves.

She'd keep at it anyway, telling them about her Spanish sailor. She was sorry now she hadn't thought of this earlier, before Mister Burgess ran away and started writing letters to everyone. It was a pity. None of this would have happened then.

—Ah cop on, Sharon, she told herself.

It was a good idea and it was working. Jackie believed her. Jackie said Mary believed her as well. Her mammy believed her. She wasn't so sure about her daddy. But she'd keep at him, telling him until she believed it herself. She'd have loved that, to believe it herself.

She'd been noticing all the Spanish students that were always upstairs on the buses at this time of year. They looked rich —their clothes were lovely —and snotty. There were a lot of fat ones. But most of them had lovely skin and hair. Black eyes and black hair.

Sharon was fair. Mister Burgess was —pink and white. His hair was like dirty water.

Maybe she should have said it was a Swedish sailor.

Too late now.

She'd have to start eating polish or something.

She grinned although she didn't really feel like it. The shampoos were done and now she crossed the aisle to the soap.

—Fuck it annyway.

The Palmolives were nearly all gone and Simple section was empty. She'd have to fill them and that meant she'd have to bend down.

* * *

It wasn't fair on the lads either, Jimmy Sr told Bimbo at his gate a few nights later, after closing time.

—I should stay at home maybe.

—Don't be thick, said Bimbo.

Jimmy Sr reckoned they'd been talking about him. He knew it. Nothing surer. Let's be nice to Jimmy. He's having it rough. Don't mention babies or Burgess or Sinbad the fuckin' Sailor. It was terrible. He'd had a good one tonight about a young lad getting up on an oul' one but he couldn't tell it. They'd have laughed too loud.

—They're just bein', eh, considerate, said Bimbo. —It'll pass.

—I suppose you're righ', said Jimmy Sr. —But I felt like a leper tonigh' the way they were smilin' at me.

—Bertie an' Paddy wouldn't smile at a leper, Jimmy. Cop on now. They just see that you're not the best these days so ——It'll pass. It'll pass. They're just bein' nice.

—I don't like them nice. I prefer them the other way; bollixes. ——Did yeh see the way the other shower were gawkin' over at me?

—Ah Jaysis, Jimmy. ——You're not startin' to get sorry for yourself, are yeh?

—Go home to bed, you.

—I will.

He yawned.

—Nigh' now, Jim.

—Good luck.

—See yeh.

Jimmy Sr had chips for Veronica but they were cold so he ate them on the step, looking across at the Burgess's, and then he went in.

* * *

It was Thursday night and Sharon was going upstairs after work. Jimmy Jr was coming down.

—Howyeh, Larry, said Sharon.

—Ah, don't start, Sharon.

—How's the practice goin'?

—Shite, to be honest with yeh. The tape sounds woeful. I sound like a fuckin' harelip. ——I'm thinkin' o' gettin' elocution lessons.

Sharon screamed.

—You!

—Yeah; why not. Don't tell Da, for fuck sake.

Sharon laughed. Jimmy grinned.

—It'd be worth it, he said, still grinning.

—How much?

—Don't know. I'm only thinkin' about it. Don't tell him but; righ'?

—Don't worry, said Sharon.

Sharon had asked about him and listened so Jimmy thought he'd better ask about her, and listen.

—How are yeh yourself an' annyway? he said.

—Grand.

—Gettin' big, wha'.

He nodded at her belly.

—Yeah, said Sharon.

—Does it hurt?

—No! ——I do exercises for the extra weight an' tha'.

—Yeah?

—Yeah. Sometimes only.

—Nothin' wrong then?

—No. Not really.

—D'yeh get sick?

—No. Not annymore.

—That's good. I was in bits meself this mornin'.

—Were yeh?

—Yeah. The oul' rum an' blacks, yeh know.

—Oh Jesus.

—I know. Never again. I puked me ring; Jesus. And me lungs. The oul' fella was batterin' the door. ——Come here, d'yeh eat annythin' funny?

—No.

—I saw yeh eatin' tha' long stuff; what's it ——celery.

—That's not funny.

—S'pose not. Never ate it.

—It's nice.

—Mickah's ma ate coal when she was havin' him.

—Jesus!

—He says annyway. She said she used to nibble it when no one was lookin'.

—That's gas ——

Jimmy looked at his watch. It wasn't there.

—Bollox! I've left me watch in work again.

—I'm goin' to me check-up tomorrow, Sharon told him.

—Yeah?

—Yeah. Me second one, it is.

—That's great. I'm —

—Not a complete physical this time. Thank God. It took fuckin' ages the first time, waitin'. They even checked me heart to see if I have a murmur.

She didn't know why she was telling Jimmy all this. She just wanted to.

—I'd a murmur once, said Jimmy. —But a lorry splat- tered it.

—Ha ha. Anyway, it's at eleven.

—Wha'?

Sharon looked at the ceiling.

—Me antenatal check-up, yeh simple-head yeh.

—Oh yeah. That's great.

He looked at where his watch usually was.

—Meetin' the lads, yeh know. See yeh, righ'.

—Yeah. See yeh.

He stopped a few steps down.

—An' come here, he said.

He was reddening a bit.

——Abou' Burgess bein' the da an' tha'.

—He's not!

—I know, I know tha'. No; I mean —IF he was.

—He's not.

—I fuckin' know. Will yeh shut up a minute. ——There's people tha' still say he is, righ'.

He was getting red again.

—An' they'll prob'ly always say it. ——I couldn't give a shite who the da is. D'yeh know what I mean?

—Yeah. ——Thanks.

—No; I wanted to say tha'. An' the lads couldn't give a fuck either.

Sharon grinned.

—Mickah says it's great.

Sharon laughed.

—He says there's hope for us all if fuckin' Burgess can —

—Jimmy!

They laughed.

—Seriously, Jimmy, though, said Sharon. —They don't really think it was him, do they?

—No, not really. It's just, yeh know —funnier.

—Yeah.

—Good luck.

He had the door open.

—Jimmy.

—Wha'?

Sharon looked over the landing rail.

—How. Now. Brown. Cow.

—Fuck off, said Jimmy Jr. —You're the only brown cow around here.

—Thanks very much!

* * *

—I'm not takin' this, said Jimmy Sr.

He pushed his chair back and stood up and walked away, towards the bar.

—What's he on abou ? Bimbo asked Bertie.

—Don't know, compadre, said Bertie.

They got up to follow Jimmy Sr.

* * *

—These are reheats, Jackie complained, but she kept eating them.

—Mine aren't too bad, said Sharon. —Look it. That's a lovely one.

She held up a huge, healthy-looking chip.

—Come here, said Jackie. —I wouldn't mind seein' tha' on a young fella.

—Jesus, Jackie!

They screamed laughing.

They were going across the Green to Jackie's house. It hadn't rained in ages so the ground was nice and hard.

—I shouldn't be eatin' these, said Sharon.

—Wha' harm can they do yeh?

—They're all fat an' things. I don't know; things that'll clog me up, I can't remember. ——She asked me did I eat chips an' tha', your woman this mornin'.

—None of her fuckin' business.

—Yeah. I said I didn't. Ah, she's nice though. She says I have the right kind o' nipples.

—Lezzer.

—Ah stop; for breast feedin'. Me blood pressure's grand.

—I'm very happy for yeh.

—Fuck off, you.

They got to Jackie's gate.

—Come here, Jackie, said Sharon. —Did Yvonne say annythin' else about me?

They'd been talking about Yvonne Burgess before they bought the chips.

—Only; she said you led him on.

—God, said Sharon. —Poor Yvonne. Still, I'll break her head for her if I see her.

—Yeh know wha' else though? said Jackie. —She said he paid yeh.

—He did, said Sharon.

Then she laughed.

Jackie looked at her, and then she laughed as well.

—I'm pissed, d'yeh know tha', said Sharon.

She patted the lodger.

—He's playin' fuckin' tennis in there.

—He's prob'ly eatin' your chips, said Jackie.

—Yeuuh; stop.

Jackie remembered what she'd wanted to ask Sharon earlier but she'd been a bit afraid to. Now, with a few vodkas inside her, she was still afraid but it was easier.

—Come here, Sharon, she said. —Why didn't yeh tell me earlier? Yeh know; abou' your sailor.

—Aah. I don't know —

Sharon couldn't tell her the truth: because I only made it up a few days ago and you ARE the first person I told. Or the realler truth: because we're not that close; or weren't anyway.

—I just ——I was too embarrassed. Sorry; I should've.

—No, it's okay. I was only —

—Here, I'll tell yeh the next time, righ'.

They screamed again, but quieter because people were in bed.

* * *

Jimmy Sr came in with a bloody nose. The blood was dry and there wasn't much of it but it was there to be seen. He put a brown paper bag with grease marks down on the table.

Veronica took off her glasses and scooped up the loose sequins and poured them into a tobacco tin. She put the lid on the tin. Then she saw Jimmy Sr and his nose.

—Where in the name of God did you get that?

—Hang on till I have a look at it, said Jimmy Sr.

He pointed at the bag.

—I got yeh a burger as well.

—You didn't go into the chipper with that nose!

—No; I got them from the van.

—You can eat them yourself then. Who hit you?

Jimmy Sr had the curtain pulled back and he was trying to get a good look at himself in the kitchen window. He was leaning over the sink.

—It doesn't look too bad. From here annyway.

—Who hit you?

Veronica was eating the chips but she wasn't going to go near the burger.

—Ah, I'll live, said Jimmy Sr.

—More's the pity, said Veronica. —Who hit you? I want to thank him.

—You would too. Are yeh not eatin' tha' burger?

The inspection was over. There was no real damage done. He hadn't even got any of it on his shirt or his jacket. He'd wash his nose before he went to bed. He took a good bite

143

out of the burger in case Veronica said, Yes, she was eating it.

—I'll tell yeh one thing though, said Jimmy Sr. —I gave back better than I got.

—Aren't you great?

—Tha' soccer shower, said Jimmy Sr. —Yeh know the bunch o' wankers tha' hang —used to hang around with Georgie Burgess. They were laughin', yeh know. The whole gang o' them. They've been at it since —yeh know. The bollixes.

—How d'you know they were laughing at you, for God's sake?

Jimmy Sr ignored the question. Bimbo had asked it already and he hadn't answered it then either.

—I got Larry O'Rourke when he was up at the bar an' I told him if, righ', if they were laughin' at me I'd fuckin' kill them. Every —

Jimmy Sr liberated the rest of the burger.

—Every —'scuse me, Veronica —every jaysis one o' them. He said they wouldn't bother their bollixes —pardon, Veronica —bother laughin' at me, an' I said they'd better not. For their own sakes.

—You're —

—An' —sorry —I gave him a bit of a dig —nothin' much now —when he was tryin' to get past me. Bimbo an' Bertie got in between us. Just as well.

He wiped his fingers with the bag.

—I'd've destroyed him.

Veronica didn't know what to say. And he was too old to be slapped.

Jimmy Sr continued.

—I'm not goin' up there annymore. I don't care. I only have to walk in an' they're —

He saw Veronica looking at him.

—I can't enjoy me pint under those conditions.

Veronica was still looking at him.

—It's fuckin' desperate, so it is.

—God almighty, said Veronica.

Jimmy Sr sat down. He tried to explain again.

—If it was annyone else. I don't care abou' the age, annyone. But Georgie Burgess! Jesus.

—Oh, shut up. I'm sick of it. Why won't you believe her?

—Oh, I do believe her. Only —I don't know. I —

They heard the door. Sharon was coming in.

—Wash your nose, said Veronica.

—There's no point.

—You want her to see it, don't you?

—That's offside, said Jimmy Sr.

It was true though.

He got up too late to be at the sink by the time Sharon came in.

—Hiyis.

—Look, Sharon, said Veronica. —Your father's been defending your honour. Isn't he great?

—What happened yeh, Daddy?

—Nothin', Sharon, nothin'. Don't listen to your mother. She's been at the sherry bottle again, ha ha.

Jimmy Sr was at the sink again. He studied the J-cloth, threw it back and rooted in his pockets for a paper hankie. He turned on the cold tap.

—Were you in a fight? Sharon asked him.

—No, no. Not really.

—He was defending your honour, I told you, said Veronica.

—Shut up, Mammy, will yeh.

—Don't —

—Shut up!

Veronica did. Sharon looked like she was going to kill Jimmy Sr and that was alright with Veronica.

Sharon was angry. Something unfair was going on.

—Wha' did yeh do? she asked Jimmy Sr.

—Ah —

—Yeah?

—They were sayin' things about yeh, Sharon, said Jimmy Sr.

His nose was clean now.

—You didn't hear them, said Veronica.

—I know wha' I heard, said Jimmy Sr. —I'm not goin' to stand by an' let annyone —annyone, I don't care who, jeer Sharon.

—You're a fuckin' eejit, Daddy, said Sharon. —Why couldn't yeh just ignore them?

—I'm not like tha', said Jimmy Sr.

He was nearly crying.

—I'm not goin' to let them jeer yeh.

He was liking himself now.

—Why not, for fuck sake?

Veronica tut-tutted.

Jimmy Sr thumped the table.

—Because you're my daughter an' —well, fuck it, you're my daughter an' as long as yeh live in this house I'm not goin' to let bollixes like them say things about yeh.

—Maybe I should leave then.

That hit like a thump.

—Ah no, Sharon.

—Maybe I will if you're goin' to get into fights all the time.

—No, Sharon, Jimmy Sr assured her. —It was just the once.

Something had gone wrong.

—I'm not goin' there again.

That wasn't the right thing to say, he realized. He changed it.

—I'm not goin' to listen to them annymore. ——They're only a shower o' shites. They're not worth it.

He felt like a right fuckin' eejit now. He couldn't look at Veronica.

—Well —, said Sharon. —Look; I know you mean well —

—I know tha', Sharon.

—I can fight my own fights, on my own.

—I know tha'.

—No better girl, said Veronica.

—Anyway, said Sharon. —They've nothin' to jeer me about. Now tha' they know I'm not havin' the baby for Mister Burgess.

—You're right o' course.

Sharon went to bed.

All Jimmy Sr had wanted was value for his nosebleed. But something had gone wrong. A bit of gratitude was all he'd expected. He'd felt noble there for a while before Sharon started talking about leaving, even though he'd been lying. But she'd attacked him instead.

There was more to it than that though.

—She put you back in your box, didn't she? said Veronica.

Veronica went to bed.

Jimmy Sr stayed there, sitting in the kitchen. He was busy admitting something: he was ashamed of Sharon. That was the problem. He was sorry for her troubles; he loved her, he was positive he did, but he was ashamed of her. Burgess! Even if there WAS a Spanish sailor ——Burgess! ——

There was something else as well: she was making an eejit of him. She wasn't doing it on purpose —there was no way she'd have got herself up the pole just to get at him. That wasn't what he meant. But, fuck it, his life was being ruined because of her. It was fuckin' terrible. He was the laughing stock of Barrytown. It wasn't her fault —but it was her fault as well. It wasn't his. He'd done nothing.

Jimmy Sr stood up. He was miserable. He'd admitted

shocking things to himself. He'd been honest. He was ashamed of Sharon. He was a louser for feeling that way but that was the way it was. He could forgive her for giving him all this grief but it would still be there after he'd forgiven her. So what was the point?

He did forgive her anyway.

A bit of gratitude would have been nice though. Not just for himself; for Veronica as well.

Jimmy Sr went up to bed.

*　*　*

Sharon nearly died.

Her heart stopped for a second. It did.

She was just getting to her gate and there was Yvonne Burgess, coming out of her house, across the road.

She must have seen her.

Sharon threw the gate out of her way and dashed up the path. She nearly went head-first through the glass in the front door. She hadn't her key with her. Oh Jesus. She rang the bell. She couldn't turn around. She rang the bell. She was bursting for the toilet. She rang the fuckin' bell. And she wanted to get sick. She rang the —The door opened. She fell in.

—I nearly gave birth in the fuckin' hall, Jackie, she said. —I'm not jokin' yeh.

*　*　*

—When will they be finished, Mammy? said Tracy.

—When they're ready, said Veronica.

—When?

—Get out.

Linda spoke.

—We have to have them —

148

—Get out!

Veronica felt Larrygogan at her feet. She gave him a kick and she didn't feel a bit guilty about it after.

*   *   *

Jimmy Sr got moodier. He wouldn't go out. He sat in the kitchen. He roared at the twins. He walloped Darren twice. He'd have hit Les as well but he didn't see Les. He stayed in bed, didn't go to work two mornings the next week. He listened to the radio and ate most of a packet of Hobnobs one of the mornings and Veronica nearly cut herself to ribbons on the crumbs when she got into bed that night. He couldn't have been that sick, she said. It wasn't his stomach that was sick, Jimmy Sr told her. What was it then? He didn't answer.

But she'd guessed it and she wanted to box his ears for him.

Jimmy Sr knew he could snap out of it but he didn't want to. He was doing it on purpose. He was protesting; that was how he described it to himself. He'd been wronged; he was suffering and he wanted them all to know this. Especially Sharon.

What he was doing was getting at Sharon. He wanted to make her feel bad, to make her realize just how much she'd hurt her father and the rest of the family.

He couldn't tell her. That wasn't the way to do it. She'd have to work it out herself —he didn't know; say Sorry or something; admit —something.

He sat in the kitchen by himself. He was dying to go in and watch a bit of the American Wrestling on the Sports Channel —he loved it; it was great gas and he always ended up feeling glad that he lived in Ireland after he'd watched it —but he didn't want them to see him enjoying himself.

He looked down at the Evening Press crossword.

8 across. Being a seaman he requires no bus. ——What did that fuckin' mean?

He looked at the pictures of the women's faces on the Dubliner's Diary page and decided how many of them he'd ride. ——All of them.

He drew moustaches on some of them, and then glasses.

Bimbo called.

—He's in the kitchen, said Darren.

—There y'are, said Bimbo.

—Howyeh, Bimbo, said Jimmy Sr. —I'm not comin' ou'.

—Ah, why not?

—Ah, said Jimmy Sr. —I'm not well. ——I'm fed up, Bimbo. I've had it up to here.

—Wha' has yeh tha' way?

—Ah —, said Jimmy Sr.

He was saying nothing.

—I know wha' you need, said Bimbo. —An' so do you. A kick up the hole an' a few nice pints.

—No way, said Jimmy Sr.

—Go on, said Bimbo. —Yeh must be constipated, yeh haven't had a pint in ages. Bertie says your shite must be brown by now.

Jimmy Sr grinned.

—Hang on till I get me jacket.

He was only human.

* * *

Sharon noticed. It wasn't hard. Her daddy stopped talking to her during the drives into work. He stopped saying Thanks Sharon when she handed him things at the table. He stopped asking her how she was and saying There's Sharon when she came in from work or in the mornings. He said Howyeh to her as if it cost him money.

At first she didn't know why. He'd been great before;

bringing her out, giving her lifts, telling her not to mind what people said. He'd helped her. He'd been brilliant. But now he didn't want anything to do with her.

It annoyed her.

She caught him looking at her belly when she turned from the cooker. She let him know he'd been snared.

—I'm gettin' very big, amn't I? she said.

—S'pose so, he answered.

That was all; no joking, no smile, not even a guilty look. He just stared at the cinema page of the Press. He never went to the pictures.

She knew now for definite what was eating him: she was. There he was, sitting there, pretending to read the paper. For a second she thought she was going to cry, but she didn't. She would have a few weeks ago, but not now. She had no problem stopping herself. A few weeks ago she wouldn't have blamed him for being like this. But —she flattened her hands on her belly —it was a bit late to be getting snotty now.

She'd have to do something.

*   *   *

What though? What could she do?

She didn't know.

But she did know that she wasn't going to put up with it. He probably didn't believe her about the sailor. Why couldn't he, the oul' bastard? Everyone else did. There was nothing she could do to make him believe her —at least she didn't think there was —but she wasn't going to let him go on treating her like shite. The twins might start copying him; and Darren. And then she'd be having the baby in —in ten weeks —Jesus —and if it didn't look a bit Spanish they'd all gang up on it before it was even fully out of her.

There was nothing in the book about snotty das. She was on her own.

She took all her clothes off and locked her parents' bedroom door and looked at herself in the wardrobe mirror and the dressing table mirror. Jesus, she looked terrible. She was white in one mirror and greeny-pink in the other one. Her tits were hanging like a cow's. They weren't anything like that before. A fella she'd gone with —Niall, a creep —once said that she should have been in the army because her tits stood to attention. She looked like a pig. In both the mirrors.

She washed her hair but the shampoo stayed in it and it looked worse. Now she wanted to cry. She tried to think of something to set her off. She thought of everything but she couldn't cry. A few drinks would have got her going; bawling. But she'd no money. And now the baby was throwing wobblers inside of her.

—Ah, lay off, will yeh, she said.

She sat down on her bed and slumped and stayed that way for ages.

*   *   *

Jimmy Sr began to time his moods. This gave him the best of both worlds. He could enjoy his depression when Sharon was around or when he thought she was around and he could enjoy his few pints with the lads as well. Sharon didn't go up to the Hikers any more —she went to Howth or Raheny or into town —so he let her believe that he didn't go there either. He didn't announce it or anything. He just hinted at it. He wondered out loud where he'd go tonight or he waited till she went out before he went out. Or he stayed in. He wanted her to think she'd robbed his local off him.

Now and again guilt got to him. He felt like a bollix and

he thought he should leave her alone and get back to normal. He'd have liked that. But every time he saw one of the soccer shower looking his way or when Georgie Burgess came into his head he decided to keep it up. Anyway, it was for her own good. She had to be made to realize all the trouble she'd caused, the consequences of her messing around.

One time at the dinner he came within that, an inch, of giving the twins a few quid to go and get choc-ices for everyone. It was a lovely day, a scorcher. But he'd stopped himself just in time.

Mind you, he bought one for himself later on his way up to the Hikers.

*　*　*

Now was as good a time as any.

—What —, Jimmy Sr started.

Bertie, Bimbo and Paddy paid attention.

—What, said Jimmy Sr, —is hard an' hairy on the outside —

Bimbo started giggling. Hairy was a great word.

—is soft an' wet on the inside —

They were laughing already.

—begins with a C —

—Oh Jaysis! said Bimbo.

—end with a T, an' has a U an' an N in it?

They sat there laughing, Jimmy Sr as well.

Paddy knew he was going to be wrong.

—A cunt, he said.

—No, said Jimmy Sr. —A coconut.

They roared.

*　*　*

—Hey Daddy, said Linda. —Will yeh watch us for a bit to tell us wha' we're doin' wrong?

Jimmy Sr looked up at her.

—Can't yeh see I'm readin' me paper? he said.

*　*　*

Veronica was looking in the dressing table mirror, hunting an eyelash that was killing her. She was leaning over the stuff on the table so she could get right in to the mirror. She saw Jimmy Sr's head floating behind her shoulder. She felt his hand go down between the cheeks of her bum. His finger pressed into her skirt.

—You're still a great lookin' —

—Get away from me, you, she barked at the mirror.

She clouted his arm with the hairbrush.

—Oh Jesus! Me fuckin' ——There was no need for tha'.

The face was gone from the mirror.

She'd been wanting to do something like that for days. Weeks.

*　*　*

Sharon asked Jackie to back her up.

—Yeah, said Jackie. —No problem.

—Is that alrigh' then?

—Yeah. It is, said Jackie. —An', come here. If nothin' happens an' he's still actin' the prick, we'll go ahead an' do it, okay?

—Are yeh serious?

—Yeah. Why not?

They were sitting in the front room of Jackie's house.

—I hate this fuckin' room, said Jackie.

Sharon laughed.

—Yeh can't open the door without trippin' over one of her ornaments, said Jackie.

* * *

He wasn't in the kitchen. She looked in the front room. He was in there by himself, watching MTV with the sound down. He only turned the sound up when he recognized the singers or when he liked the look of them. Veronica had been in bed since just after the tea. It had been a bad day. The twins and Darren were in bed. The twins were asleep. Darren was listening to Bon Jovi on Jimmy Jr's walkman. Jimmy would kill him when he caught him but it was worth it: Bon Jovi were brilliant. Jimmy Jr was in Howth, trying to get into Saints. Mickah Wallace was with him so it wasn't easy. Les was out. Larrygogan was in the coal shed.

Jimmy Sr didn't go to bed these days until Sharon got in.

—Hiyeh, said Sharon.

Jimmy Sr didn't answer. He kept his eyes on Curiosity Killed the Cat.

—I said Hiyeh, Daddy, said Sharon.

—I heard yeh.

—Then why didn't yeh answer me?

—Wait a —

—An' why haven't yeh answered for the last —weeks?

She got the pouffe and sat in front of him.

—You're in me way, look it, he said.

She said it louder.

—Why haven't yeh answered me?

—Get lost, will yeh; I have.

Jimmy Sr'd been taken by surprise. He tried to look around Sharon. She leaned back —it wasn't easy —and turned off the telly.

—Yeh haven't, she said. —Yeh haven't said hello to me properly in ages.

Jimmy Sr was never going to admit anything like that.

—You're imaginin' things, he said.

—No, I'm not.

She looked straight at him. There wasn't any shaking in her voice. She just spoke. She was a bit frightening.

—I'll tell yeh the last time yeh spoke to me.

—I said hello to yeh yesterday.

—Yeh didn't. Not properly. The last time yeh said hello to me properly was before the night yeh got hit in the nose.

—Now listen; that's not true.

—It is. An' you know it.

Jimmy Sr wondered if he'd be able to get past her and up to bed. He thought she was capable of trying to stop him.

—Are yeh goin' to tell me why? Sharon asked him.

He looked as if he was going to get up. She didn't know what she'd do if he did that. She'd follow him.

—There's nothin' to tell, for fuck sake, said Jimmy Sr.

—It's me, isn't it?

—Go up to bed, will yeh.

—It is, said Sharon. —I can tell.

Sharon nearly had to stop herself from grinning as she asked the next question.

—Did I do somethin' to yeh?

Jesus, she was asking him had she done something: had she done something! She could sit there and —

—You've done nothin', Sharon.

—I'll tell yeh what I've done.

Her voice had softened. The bitch; he couldn't have a proper row with her that way.

—I'm pregnant. ——I saw yeh lookin' at me.

Jimmy Sr said nothing yet.

—I've disgraced the family.

—No.

—Don't bother denyin' it, Daddy. I'm not givin' out.

The look on his face gave her the sick for a minute.

—I've been stupid, she said. —An' selfish. I should've known. An' I know tha' you still think it was Mister Burgess an' that makes it worse.

—I don't think it was —

—Ah ah! she very gently gave out to him. ——You were great. Yeh did your best to hide it.

—Ah, Sharon —

—If I leave it'll be the best for everyone. Yeh can get back to normal.

—Leave.

—Yeah. Leave. Go. Yeh know what I mean.

She stopped herself from getting too cheeky.

—I'm only bringin' trouble for you an' Mammy, so I'm ——Me an' Jackie are goin' to get a flat. Okay?

—You're not goin'?

—I am. I want to. It's the best. Nigh' night.

She went upstairs.

—Ah Sharon, no.

Sharon got undressed. She wondered if it would work; what he was thinking; was he feeling guilty or what. The face on him when she was talking to him; butter wouldn't melt in his fuckin' mouth, the bastard. She got into bed. She wondered if she'd be here next week. God, she hoped so. She didn't want to move into a flat, even with Jackie. She'd seen some. She didn't want to be by herself, looking after herself and the baby. She wanted to stay here so the baby would have a proper family and the garden and the twins and her mammy to look after it so she could go out sometimes. She didn't want to leave. What was he thinking down there?

Jimmy Sr sat back and stretched.

Victory: he'd won. Without having to admit anything himself, he'd got her to admit that she was the one in the wrong. She was to blame for all this, and he'd been great. She'd said it herself.

Jimmy Sr stretched further and sank down in the couch. He punched his fists up into the air.

—Easy! Easy! he roared quietly.

He'd won. He'd got what he wanted.

—Here we go, here we go, here we go!

He stood up.

He could get back to normal now. He'd drive her all the way to work on Monday, right up to the door. He'd bring her out for a drink at tea-time on Sunday, up to the Hikers. He'd insist.

He switched on the telly to have a quick look and see if there was a good video on. There was a filthy one they sometimes showed after midnight. No; it was only some shower of wankers running down a beach. He switched it off.

He was glad it was over. He preferred being nice. It was easier.

Sharon had been great there, the way she'd taken the blame. Fair play to her. She was a great young one; the way she'd just sat there and said her bit, and none of the fuckin' water works that you usually got. Any husband of Sharon's would have his work cut out for him.

Tomorrow he'd tell her not to leave.

* * *

He told her when she came down for her breakfast. Veronica was there too but she was determined not to have anything to do with it. She was sick of the two of them.

—No, Daddy, said Sharon. —Thanks, but I've made me mind up.

—But there's no need, Sharon.

—No; you've been great. So have you, Mammy.

—I know.

—Hang on, Veronica; this is serious. You can't go, Sharon. I won't let yeh.

—Try fuckin' stoppin' me.

—Now there's no need for tha' now. We want yeh to stay here with us an' have it —

He nodded and pointed.

—the baby there, with us. Don't we?

Veronica didn't look up from Tracy's ballroom dress.

—Yes, she said.

Sharon stopped spreading the Flora on her brownbread.

—I'm goin'.

Jimmy Sr believed her.

—When?

—After dinner.

—Wha'!? Today?

—Yeah.

—Ah, for fuck sake, Sharon —

Jimmy Jr walked in. He wasn't looking the best. He headed for the fridge.

—Why aren't you in work? said Jimmy Sr.

—Wha'?

Jimmy Jr's head came out of the fridge.

—It's alrigh'. I'll phone in. I'll work me day off. Is there anny Coke?

—No.

—Or annythin' with bubbles in it?

—Go down to the shops, said Veronica.

—I'd never make it.

He sat down carefully and stared at the table.

Sharon was cursing him. Now she'd have to start again.

—It's the best thing to do, she said.

—What's tha'? said Jimmy Sr. —No. Fuck it, Sharon; this is your home.

His voice didn't sound right. It was shivery. He coughed.

—You should stay —stay with your family.

Sharon smiled.

—Now maybe. But, look it.

She patted her belly.

—It's goin' to be gettin' bigger an' yeh won't be able to get out of its way an' stop lookin' at it. It'll keep remindin' you of Mister Burgess. No, it will; even though he's not —So, yeh see, it's best for us all if I go.

She stood up. She smiled. She patted his shoulder.

—I'll go upstairs an' pack.

Jimmy Sr was afraid to say anything. He didn't know what it would sound like. He'd never felt like this before.

Sharon was planking going up the stairs. She hoped she hadn't been too convincing. He mightn't bother trying to stop her. She didn't even have a suitcase or anything. She'd just pile her stuff on the bed.

Jimmy Sr didn't know what to do. It was terrible. Sharon was leaving because of him. That wasn't what he'd wanted at all.

It was wrong.

Jimmy Jr's face distracted him.

—Jaysis, he said.

Jimmy Jr was still staring at the table. Veronica looked up from the dress.

—Get up, quick!

Jimmy Jr stood up and fell across to the sink. He dropped his head and vomited —HYUHH —uh —— fuck —— HYY— —YUUH! —onto the breakfast plates and cups.

That was it, Jimmy Sr decided. There was no way Sharon could go. She was the only civilized human being in the whole fuckin' house.

Veronica had her face in her hands. She shook her head slowly.

Jimmy Sr stood up.

—Veronica, he said. —She's not goin'.

Veronica looked up at him. She still had her hands to her face but she nodded.

—An' come here, you, he bawled across to Jimmy Jr. —Wash up them dishes, righ'.

Jimmy Jr groaned.

Sharon heard the stairs creaking. She threw a bundle of knickers onto the bed.

Jimmy Sr knocked, and came in.

—Are you alone?

—Yeah.

—Where're the twins?

—Camogie, I think.

—They do everythin', don't they?

—Yeah.

—Fair play to them. Don't go, Sharon.

—I have to.

She stopped messing with the clothes.

—Yeh don't have to ——

Jimmy Sr looked across, out the window. His eyes were shiny. He kept blinking. He gulped, but the lump kept rising.

—I'm cryin', Sharon, sorry. I didn't mean to.

He pulled the sleeve of his jumper over his fist and wiped his eyes with it.

—Sorry, Sharon.

He looked at her. She looked as if she didn't know how she should look, what expression she should have on.

—Em —I don't know wha' to fuckin' say. ——That's the first time I cried since your granny died. Hang on; no. I didn't cry then. I haven't cried since I was a kid.

—You cried last Christmas.

—Sober, Sharon. Drunk doesn't count. We all do stupid things when we're drunk.

—I know.

—Fuck, sorry; I didn't mean it like tha'!

He looked scared.

—I know tha', said Sharon.

—Sorry. ——Annyway, look —I've been a righ' bollix, Sharon. I've made you feel bad an' that's why you're leavin'. Just cos I was feelin' hard done by. It's my fault. Don't go, Sharon. Please.

Sharon was afraid to say no. She didn't want to start him crying again.

—But I'll only keep remindin' yeh —

—Sorry, Sharon. For interruptin' yeh. ——This isn't easy for me. I wanted to make you feel bad cos I was feelin' sorry for myself. I can't look at yeh, sayin' this. It's very fuckin' embarrassin'.

He tried to grin but he couldn't.

—I behaved like a bollix, I realize tha' now. ——I didn't think you'd leave. Don't leave. We need you here. Your mammy —Your mammy's not always the best. Because of —Yeh know tha' yourself. I'm a fuckin' waster. Jimmy's worse. D'yeh know what he's at now?

—Wha'?

—He's down there gettin' sick into the sink. On top o' the plates an' stuff.

—Oh my God.

—Poor Veronica. ——The fuckin' dinner might be —what's the word —steepin' in the sink for all I know. Believe me, Sharon, we need you. The twins, they need you.

Sharon was nearly crying now. She was loving this.

—What abou' the baby?

Jimmy Sr breathed deeply and looked out the window, and looked at Sharon. His eyes were shiny again.

—I feel like a fuckin' eejit. ——I love you, Sharon. An' it'll be your baby, so I'll love it as well.

—Wha' —what if it looks like Mister Burgess?

Jimmy Sr creased his forehead. Then he spoke.

—I don't mind what it looks like. I don't give a shite.

—It's easy to say tha' now —

—I don't, Sharon, I swear I don't. Not now, fuck it. I don't mind. If the first words it says are On the Bible, Jim, on the Bible, I won't mind. I'll still love it.

Sharon was laughing.

—If it looks like Burgess's arse I'll love it, Sharon. On the Bible.

They were both laughing. They'd both won. Both sets of eyes were watery. Sharon spoke.

—What if it's a girl an' she looks like Mister Burgess?

—Ah well, fuck it; we'll just have to smother it an' leave it on his step.

—Ah Daddy!

—I'm only messin'. I suppose I'll still have to love her. Even if she does have a head on her like Georgie Bur —

He couldn't finish. He had an almighty fit of the giggles.

—She'll be lovely, said Sharon.

—She'd fuckin' better be. We're a good lookin' family. 'Cept for Jimmy, wha'. An', come here, an' anyway; it won't look like Burgess cos he isn't the da. ——Isn't tha' righ'?

—Yeah.

—Unless your Spanish sailor looked a bit like him, did he?

——Just a little bit.

—Ah well, said Jimmy Sr after a small while. —Your poor mammy. I'd better go down an' see if your man's still spinnin' the discs in the sink. ——Good girl, Sharon.

—See yeh in a minute. I'll just put me stuff back.

—Good girl.

He was gone, but he came back immediately.

—Eh, sorry; Sharon?

—Yeah?

—Don't tell Jimmy yeh saw me cryin' there, sure yeh won't?

—Don't worry.

—Good girl.

He grinned.

—He looks up to me, yeh know.

* * *

—Ah, said Jimmy Sr to the twins. —There yis are. An' there's Larry with yis.

He bent down and patted the dog's head.

—He's growin', he said. —He'll soon be makin' his communion. Yis must be thirsty after your camogie, are yis?

—Yeah, said Linda and Tracy.

—Yes! said Veronica.

—Yes, said Linda.

—There, said Jimmy Sr.

It was a pound.

—Get yourselves some 7 Ups. Or the one tha' Tina Turner drinks. Pepsi.

—What about me?

—A Toblerone?

—And a Flake.

Jimmy Sr's hand went back into his pocket.

—Can we have a Flake instead of the 7 Up? said Tracy.

—No! ——Oh, alrigh'.

The twins legged it.

Jimmy Sr smiled over at Veronica.

—Are yeh well, Veronica?

—I'm alright, said Veronica.

—Good, said Jimmy Sr. —Good.

* * *

It was a few weeks later.

Jimmy Sr dropped the book onto the couch. He was the only one in the front room.

—Wha' in the name o' Jaysis was tha'? he said out loud to himself although he knew what it was.

Veronica had just screamed. What Jimmy Sr really wanted to know was, why? He struggled out of the couch. It hadn't sounded like a scream of pain or shock. It'd been more of a roar.

—No peace in this fuckin' house, he sort of muttered as he went down to the kitchen.

Tracy and Linda were in there with Veronica.

—What's goin' on here? said Jimmy Sr.

He saw the way Veronica was glaring at the twins and the twins were trying to glare back, keeping the table between themselves and their mother. They looked at Jimmy Sr quickly, then back at Veronica in case she did something while they were looking at Jimmy Sr.

—What's wrong? said Jimmy Sr.

Veronica picked up the dress from her lap and clutched it in front of her, nearly hard enough to tear it.

—Are you after upsettin' your mammy? said Jimmy Sr.

—No, said Linda.

—No, said Tracy.

Jimmy Sr was going to shout at them.

—We on'y told her somethin', said Linda. —Tracy said it.

—You did as well! said Tracy.

—Shut up! Jimmy Sr roared.

They jumped. They didn't know where to move. If they got away from their daddy that would mean getting closer to their mammy and she had the scissors on the table in front of her.

Veronica spoke.

—All those ——fuckin' sequins, she said, softly. —Oh my sweet Jesus.

Jimmy Sr could have murdered Linda and Tracy. They

saw this, so they both answered promptly when he asked them what they'd said to their mother.

—Tracy said —

—Linda said I was —

—Shut up!

Tracy started crying.

Jimmy Sr pointed at Linda.

—Tell me.

—Tracy said —

Jimmy Sr's pointed finger seemed to get closer to her although he didn't move. She started again.

—We on'y told her we weren't doin' the dancin' annymore.

—Oh good fuck, said Jimmy Sr, not loudly.

He looked at Veronica. She was staring at a little pile of sequins in front of her.

—Yis ungrateful little brassers, he said.

—It's stupid, said Linda. —I'm sick of it. It's stupid.

Veronica came back to life.

—They're not giving it up, she said.

—That's righ'.

—Ah Mammy —

—No! said Veronica.

—But it's stupid.

—You heard your mammy, didn't yeh? said Jimmy Sr.
—DIDN'T YEH?

——Yeah.

—An' wha' did she say?

———

—ANSWER ME.

——We have to keep doin' it.

—That's righ', said Jimmy Sr. —An', what's more, yis'll enjoy it. An' if I hear anny whingin' out o' yis yis'll need an operation to get my foot ou' of your arses. ——Now, say you're sorry.

——Sorry.

—Not to me.

——Sorry.

—Now go inside an' practise, said Jimmy Sr.

They got past Jimmy Sr without touching him. He heard Tracy when they'd got out of the kitchen.

—I don't care, I'm not doin' it.

Jimmy Sr rushed out and grabbed her and, without intending to, lifted her.

—Wha' did you say?

—Aah! —Nothin'!

—Are yeh sure?

She was rubbing her arm and deciding whether to cry or not.

—Yeah, she said.

—Good, said Jimmy Sr. —Now get in there an' cha cha cha.

Darren was coming in the back door when Jimmy Sr got back to the kitchen.

—Again? said Jimmy Sr.

—Yeah, said Darren.

He'd crashed again. One side of his face was grazed, the darkest, reddest scrape along his cheekbone.

—Look.

Darren showed them where his jersey was ripped.

—Look it.

He showed them the big, wide scrape down his leg. He was delighted.

Jimmy Sr remembered having a gash like that, only bigger, when he was a young fella. He was going to tell Darren about it but he decided not to, not with Veronica there.

—Wha' happened yeh? he said instead.

Sharon came in from work.

—Hiyis.

—There's Sharon. Do us a favour, love. Talk to the twins, will yeh. ——They're talkin' abou' wantin' to give up the oul' dancin', yeh know?

He nodded at Veronica. Sharon looked at her.

—Okay, she said.

—Good girl. They're in with the telly. Practisin'.

Sharon saw Darren.

—God, wha' happened yeh?

—I came off me bike.

He smiled.

—Sharon'll sort them ou', Jimmy Sr told Veronica.

—Are we havin' the dinner?

Veronica put the dress on the table. She stood up and looked around her, as if she'd just woken up with a fright.

—It'll have to be from the chipper, she said.

—Grand, said Jimmy Sr. —Darren can go an' show off his war wounds, wha'.

Darren laughed.

—How'd it happen? Jimmy Sr asked him.

—I was blemmin' down Tonlegee Road.

—Jaysis! Was it a race?

—Yeah, but I didn't give up. I got on again an' I finished it.

—Good man, said Jimmy Sr. —Course yeh did. Did yeh win?

—No. I was last but Mister Cantwell says I showed the righ' spirit.

—He's dead righ'.

He turned to Veronica.

—Just like his da, wha'.

He turned back to Darren.

—Did yeh know I met your mammy when I fell off me bike?

—Did yeh?

—He was drunk, said Veronica.

—It was love, said Jimmy Sr. —Love knocked me off me
bike.

Darren spoke.

—Mister Cantwell says we're not to bother with young
ones cos they'll only distract us.

Jimmy Sr laughed.

—Fair play to Mister Cantwell. He's dead righ'.
——Cantwell. He's your man from across from the shops,
isn't he?

—Yeah.

—He does the church collection.

—Yeah.

—Isn't he great? said Veronica.

Jimmy Sr grinned at her.

—An' he's your manager, is he?

—Yeah.

—Good. What're yis called?

—The Barrytown Cyclin' Club.

—Go 'way! That's very clever.

—Don't mind him, Veronica told Darren. —He's just
being smart. Wash your cuts and then you're to go to the
chipper.

—I don't need to wash —

—Do wha' your mammy tells yeh.

Darren did.

Jimmy Sr looked at Veronica.

—How're yeh feelin', love?

—Ah ——

Linda and Tracy came in.

—Yes? said Jimmy Sr.

The twins looked at each other. Then Linda spoke.

—Ma, we're sorry.

—Mammy.

—Mammy. We're sorry.

—It's not tha' bad, said Tracy. —It's not really stupid.

—Won't yeh keep makin' our dresses? said Linda.

—She will o' course, said Jimmy Sr.

—I'll think about it, said Veronica to Jimmy Sr.

—She'll think abou' it, said Jimmy Sr.

He clapped his hands.

—The few chips'll go down well, he said.

He went over to the bread bin.

—I'll butter a few slices, will I? For butties.

—You think of nothing except your stomach, said Veronica.

—It's the family's stomachs I'm thinkin' of, Veronica, me dear.

He rolled up two slices and shoved them into his mouth. He winked at Veronica and then he went back to the front room. Sharon was in there, alone. She was sitting on the couch, and reading Jimmy Sr's book.

—Who's readin' this? she asked Jimmy Sr when she saw him.

He shouldn't have left it there.

—I am, he said.

—You!

The book was Everywoman.

—Yeah. ——Why not?

He sat down beside her.

—What're yeh readin' it for? Sharon asked him.

—Aah ——Curiosity. I suppose.

—Where d'yeh get it?

—Library.

He looked at Sharon. He took the book from her.

—I didn't know there was so much to it, yeh know.

—Yeah.

—It's like the inside of a fuckin' engine or somethin'. 'Cept engines don't grow.

Sharon grinned.

—D'yeh get cramps, Sharon? said Jimmy Sr.

Sharon laughed a bit.

—No. Not yet annyway.

—Good. Good. I'd say they'd be a killer. We'll have to keep our fingers crossed. ——Anythin' else?

—Wrong?

—Yeah.

—No.

—Good. That's good.

—I went to me antenatal check-ups.

—Yeh did o' course. ——An' wha' were they like?

—Grand.

—Good. ——Good. Darren's gone to the chipper, for the dinners.

—Yeah.

—That's some knock he got.

—Yeah.

—He got up though, fair play to him. ——I was lookin' at another chapter there.

He opened the book and closed it and opened it again and looked at a diagram and closed it.

—The one abou' ——doin' the business, yeh know.

—Sex?

—Yeah. Exactly. ——Jaysis, I don't know —It's very fuckin' complicated, isn't it?

Sharon laughed, and felt her face getting hot.

—I can't say I don't know, she said.

—Wha'? Oh yeah. ——I'd say Georgie Burgess was a dab hand at the oul' —wha' d'yeh macall it —the foreplay, wha'?

—Daddy!

—Sorry. Sorry, Sharon. It wasn't Burgess, I know. I just said it for a laugh. But ——abou', yeh know, ridin' an' tha' —I thought it was just ——D'yeh know wha' I mean?

—I think so.

—Jaysis, Sharon. I don't know —

—I'd better warn Mammy.

—Wha'? Oh yeah. Very good. Yeah. ——Annyway, I was lookin' at another bit here. Look it.

Les saved Sharon by sticking his head round the door. Jimmy Sr felt the draught and looked up.

—Jaysis!

—Howyeh.

—Leslie. How are yeh?

—Alrigh'.

—Good man. How're the jobs goin'?

—Alrigh'.

—Good man. Gardens?

—Yeah.

—An' windows.

—Yeah.

—Good. Gives yeh a few bob annyway, wha'. Are yeh havin' your dinner with us?

—Yeah.

—My God. We'll have to kill the fatted cod for yeh.

—Wha'?

—Darren's gone to the chipper.

—He's back.

—Is he?

—Yeah.

—Why didn't yeh tell us? I'm fuckin' starvin'. ——Hang on.

He took the book.

—I'll put this upstairs, he said to Sharon. —I wouldn't want Darren to see it. ——Or Jimmy.

Sharon laughed.

—I could blackmail yeh now.

—Yeh could indeed. Yeh could alrigh'.

* * *

They heard the radio being turned up.

—Righ' now, said Jimmy Sr. —Listen now.

He looked up at the ceiling. Sharon and Veronica looked up at the ceiling.

Alison Moyet was singing Is This Love. The sound dropped.

—Now, said Jimmy Sr.

They listened.

—THIS IS JOMMY ROBBITTE − ALL − OVER − ORELAND.

Then the sound went up again.

—There, said Jimmy Sr. —Doesn't he sound different?

* * *

—Sorry, Sharon, said Jimmy Sr. —Sorry for interruptin' yeh.

Sharon wasn't doing anything really. She hadn't the energy even to get up. She was lying on the couch, flicking through the channels.

Jimmy Sr was at the door.

—Wha'? said Sharon.

She was getting really tired of her da; all his questions.

—How many weeks are yeh pregnant, exactly? said Jimmy Sr.

—Thirty-five. Why?

—Just checkin'.

—What're yeh lookin' at?

—Your ankles. They don't look too swollen.

—They're not.

—Good.

Sharon hoped that was that.

It wasn't.

—I was just readin' there, said Jimmy Sr. —Abou' what's goin' on, yeh know. It made me a bit worried.

Sharon said nothing. She flicked to BBC 2; two hippies talking.

—Pain is mentioned a bit too often for my likin'. ——Are yeh in pain, Sharon?

—No.

—None?

—No.

—At all?

—No!

—Good. ——I'll leave yeh to your telly. Sorry for disturbin' yeh.

—Okay.

He was becoming a right pain in the neck. He'd be down again in a few minutes with more questions. Last night he'd told Darren and the twins to get out of the room and then he asked her if her shite was lumpy!

He came home earlier in the week with two new pillows for her so she could prop herself up in bed.

—It'll take some o' the pressure off the oul' diaphram, Sharon.

Was she in pain, he asked her. The fuckin' eejit; she'd give him pain if he didn't get off her case. It was her pregnancy and he could fuck off and stay out of it. If he came in once more, once more she'd —

She felt fuckin' terrible.

The screen became blurred.

She was sweating and wet and she'd gone over herself with the hairdryer an hour ago only and she was still sweating and wet. Her hair was dead and manky. She could hardly walk. She was really hot and full; full like the way she used to be on Christmas Day when she was a kid; stuffed. It was brutal. She was a fat wagon, that was what she was.

She hoped Jackie'd call down because she wanted to see

her but she couldn't be bothered getting up. ——She'd been like this all her life.

Ah fuck it; she tried to get up.

The heat made her sleepy. She hated sleeping this way. It wasn't right. Only oul' ones did it.

She thought she heard her daddy's voice.

—Good girl, Sharon.

* * *

—What d'you think you're doing down there? Veronica asked Jimmy Sr.

—Hang on a minute. ——How's tha', Veronica?

—I'm cold. ——Aah!

—What's wrong?

—Your fingernail! Get up here; I'm freezing.

—Okay. ——I love you, Veronica.

—Jesus. Get out and brush your teeth. No; hang on. Do that again.

—Wha'? Tha'?

—Yeah.

—There. D'yeh like tha', Veronica?

—It's alright.

She grabbed his hair.

—Where did you learn it?

—Ah, let go!

—Where!?

—In a buke! Let go o' me!

* * *

Her face was wet. She pushed the blanket and the sheet off and the nice cool air hit her and made her feel awake, and that was what she wanted.

Bits of the dream clung. She'd had a miscarriage, in an

empty bath. She kept having miscarriages; like going to the toilet. And they all lived, hundreds of them, all red and raw and folded over. All crawling all over her. And she lay there and more of them climbed out of her.

It was only half-five but she got out of bed. By the time she'd got downstairs to the kitchen her head was clear and the dream wasn't part of her any more. She just remembered it. It was stupid.

She hadn't thought about what the baby would be like before; only if it would be a boy or a girl. God, she hoped it would be normal and healthy and then she nearly stopped breathing when she realized she'd just thought that. What if it wasn't? Jesus. What if it was deformed, or retarded like Missis Kelly's baby down the road; what then? And she'd been worrying that it might look like Mister Burgess!

She was kind of looking forward to being a mother but if —

The kettle was boiling.

It might be a Down's Syndrome baby. It would never be able to do anything for itself. It wouldn't grow properly. It would have that face, that sort of face they all had.

The baby nudged her.

She'd seen a programme about dwarfs. It said that there were ten thousand of them in Britain. The ones on the programme seemed happy enough.

She started laughing. She'd suddenly seen her mammy making a ballroom dress for a dwarf.

This was stupid. If she kept on like this something was bound to go wrong. That was what always happened.

It had gone wrong already —it was too late —if anything HAD gone wrong, if there was something wrong with it.

She spread her hands over her dressing gown.

What was in there?

The baby bounced gently off the wall of her uterus. She opened her dressing gown and put her hands back on her belly. It moved again, like a dolphin going through the water; that was the way she imagined it.

—Are yeh normal? she said.

She wished to fuck it was all over. She was sick of it, and worried sick as well.

—Soon, she said.

*　*　*

—Specially with a few chips, said Bertie.

They howled.

—I'm fuckin' serious, righ', said Jimmy Sr.

He was getting furious.

—It IS a fuckin' miracle.

—Fuckin' sure it is, Your Holiness, said Paddy.

Bimbo was wiping his eyes.

—You're a sick bunch o' fuckers, said Jimmy Sr.

Bertie pointed at Jimmy Sr, and sang.

—MOTHER OF CHRIST —

STAR OF THE SEA—

Jimmy Sr mashed a beer mat.

*　*　*

—Sharon, said Jimmy Sr.

Sharon looked up from her Bella.

Not again.

—Yeah? she said.

—D'yeh know your hormones?

—Wha'?

—Your hormones, said Jimmy Sr.

Sharon was interested.

—What abou' them?

—Are they givin' yeh anny trouble?

—Eh ——wha' d'yeh mean?

—Well —

He shifted his chair.

—I was just readin' there yesterday abou' how sometimes your hormones start actin' up when you're pregnant an' tha'. An' yis get depressed or, eh, snotty or —yeh know?

Sharon said nothing. She didn't know she'd been asked a question.

—Don't get me wrong now, Sharon, said Jimmy Sr. —Hormonal changes are perfectly normal. Part an' parcel of the pregnancy, if yeh follow me. But sometimes, like, there are side effects. Snottiness or depression or actin' a bit queer.

—I'm grand, said Sharon.

—Good, said Jimmy Sr. —Good girl. That's good. I thought so myself. I just wanted to be on the safe side, yeh know.

—Yeah, said Sharon. —No, I'm grand. I feel fine. I'd another check-up. Me last one, I think.

—An' no problems?

—No.

—Good. All set so.

Sharon got back to her magazine, but Jimmy Sr wasn't finished yet.

—I was lookin' at this other buke there an' ——It was abou' wha' happens —

He pointed at the table, just in front of Sharon.

—inside in the woman for the nine months. The pictures. Fuckin' hell; I don't know how they do it. There was this one o' the foetus, righ'. That's the name o' —

—I know what it is, Daddy!

—Yeh do o' course. ——I'm a stupid thick sometimes.

—Ah, you're not.

—Ah, I am. Annyway, it was only seven weeks, Sharon. Seven weeks. In colour, yeh know. It had fingers —

He showed her his fingers.

—Ah, Jaysis, everythin'. An' the little puss on him, yeh know.

—Yeah, it's incredible, isn't it?

—It fuckin' is, said Jimmy Sr. ——It got me thinkin'. I know it sounds stupid but —

He was blushing. But he looked straight at her.

—Youse were all like tha' once, said Jimmy Sr. —Yeh know. Even Jimmy. ——I was as well long, long ago.

He belched.

—'Scuse me, Shar —

He belched again.

—Sharon. Tha' fried bread's a killer. ——Wha' I'm tryin' to say is ——when yeh look at tha' picture, righ', an' then the later ones, an' then the born baby growin' up —Well, it's a fuckin' miracle, isn't it?

—I s'pose it is, said Sharon.

—It's got to be, said Jimmy Sr. —Shhh!

Veronica came back into the kitchen. She'd been upstairs, lying down.

—There's Veronica, said Jimmy Sr. —Yeh may as well fill the oul' kettle while you're on your feet.

—God almighty, said Veronica. —You'd die of the thirst before you'd get up and do it yourself.

—That's not true, said Jimmy Sr. —I'd say I'd've got up after a while.

The front door was opened and slammed. Jimmy Jr came in from work.

—Hoy, said Jimmy Jr.

Jimmy Sr studied him.

—Ahoy, he said. —Shiver me timbers. It's Jim lad, me hearties. Hoy! Is there somethin' wrong with your mouth?

—Fuck off.

—That's better.

—Fuck off.

—Better still. Ahoy, Veronica. There's the kettle.

—I'll get it, said Sharon.

—Now don't be ——Only if you're makin' one for yourself now.

Jimmy Sr looked up at Jimmy Jr. Then he sang.

—JUST A MINUTE —

THE SIXTY SECOND QUIZ —.

—Fuck off.

—That's lovely language from a DJ.

The front room door opened and they heard the music of Victor Sylvester and his orchestra.

—Ah now, said Jimmy Sr. —There's music. Listen to tha', wha'.

He tapped the table.

—Oh my Jaysis, said Jimmy Jr. —This is embarrassin'.

Sharon laughed. Veronica smiled. Jimmy Sr closed his eyes and nodded his head and kept tapping the table.

Linda and Tracy had danced into the hall. Sharon and Veronica went to the door to watch them.

—They're very good, aren't they? said Sharon. —You can nearly hear their bones clickin' when they turn like tha'.

Jimmy Sr was impressed.

—They're good enough for the Billie Barry kids, he said. —Too fuckin' good.

They heard the doorbell.

Linda came running down, into the kitchen.

—Da, Mister Cantwell wants yeh.

—Cantwell? Wha' does he want?

He stood up.

—Don't know, said Linda.

—It must be abou' Darren. Where is he?

—He's out, said Veronica.

—Oh God.

Jimmy Sr dashed out to the front door. The others stayed where they were.

—Hope he's not hurt, said Sharon.

—Shut up, for God's sake! said Veronica.

She sat down and lined up a row of sequins.

Victor Sylvester was still playing

Jimmy Sr came back. He was pale.

—What did he want; what's wrong?

—Wha'? said Jimmy Sr. —Oh. It wasn't abou' Darren. Is Leslie in?

—Don't be stupid.

They all relaxed, except Jimmy Sr. He put a painted cement gnome on the table.

—Ah, look it, said Tracy.

—He says tha' Leslie threw tha' thing through his window. His, eh, drawin' room window.

They all studied the gnome. It had a red cap and trousers and a yellow beard. Jimmy Jr laughed.

—Don't start, said Jimmy Sr. —It's not funny. ——Would Leslie do tha'?

—Did he see him?

—No.

—Well then.

—Did he dust it for fingerprints? said Jimmy Jr.

—Wha'? ——Oh yeah. No. He says he'll let me deal with it this time but if it happens again he'll have to get the guards. He said Leslie's always hangin' around outside his house. Loiterin', he said.

—Did you not say annythin' back? said Sharon.

—I know wha' yeh mean, said Jimmy Sr. —I should've. He's no proof. I'll go round an' have it ou' with him later. On me way to the Hikers. But, he explained, —I got a terrible fuckin' fright.

They waited for more.

—Look at its face, said Jimmy Sr.

They did.

—It's the spit o' George Burgess.

It was.

* * *

Darren had news for them the next day at tea time.

—Pat Burgess said his da's after comin' back.

Jimmy Sr put his knife and fork down.

—I knew it, he said. —I fuckin' knew it. I told yis. When I saw tha' gnome yoke's face. ——Where is it?

—Out on the windowsill, said Veronica.

—Well, it's goin' in the bin the minute I've liberated these fishfingers.

He shovelled one into him.

—So he's back, he said.

He looked at Sharon.

—I don't care, she said.

—Good girl, said Jimmy Sr. —Course yeh don't. He's only a bollix, isn't tha' righ'?

—Yeah.

* * *

Darren had more news later.

—I've been dropped.

He sat down on the arm of the couch and looked like he'd just seen his dog being splattered.

—From the soccer? said Jimmy Sr.

—No, said Darren.

Fuck the soccer, his face said.

—The cyclin'.

—Ah no. Why?

—Cos —cos you won't pay for Mister Cantwell's window an' yeh called him names.

—I didn't call him names, said Jimmy Sr.

—You told me you called him a little Virgin Mary, said Veronica.

—Now, Veronica. Please. ——Let me talk to Darren.

Darren couldn't stop the tears any more.

—Why won't yeh pay him? he asked Jimmy Sr.

—Why should I? said Jimmy Sr. —Listen, Darren; he's lookin' for twenty-five quid an' he doesn't even know for definite tha' Leslie broke the window. He only thinks he did. D'yeh expect me to cough up every time the man thinks Leslie done somethin'?

—All ——all I know is —

—Ah Darren, sorry. But it's a matter o' principle. I can't pay him. It's not the money —

—It is!

—It isn't! ——It's not the money, Darren. Fuck the money. It's the principle o' the thing. If he even said he saw Leslie runnin' away I'd pay him. But Leslie says he didn't do it an', fuck it, I believe him.

Darren's voice hurt Jimmy Sr.

—I'll never get back on the team now.

Jimmy Sr thought about this. Darren was probably right. He didn't know Cantwell but he looked like that sort of a small-minded bollix.

—We'll form our own club.

—Wha'?

—We'll form our own fuckin' club, said Jimmy Sr.

He laughed and rubbed his hands and looked around him, laughing.

—You're messin', said Darren.

—I'm not, Darren, I can assure you. I've been thinkin' that I should get involved in somethin' ——for the kids ——an' the community.

—Oh my God, said Veronica.

—A cyclin' club, Darren. Wha' d'yeh say?

—Are yeh not messin'?

—I'm deadly serious, said Jimmy Sr. —Cross me heart, look it, an' hope to die. You are attendin' the inaugural meetin' of the new cyclin' club.

—Wha'?

—This is the club's first meetin'.

Darren studied his da's face.

—Ahh, rapid!

Jimmy Sr beamed.

—Is tha' alrigh' then? he asked.

—Ah Da; yeah. Fuckin' —sorry —brilliant!

Veronica was pretending to watch Today Tonight.

—Darren's joined a new club, Veronica, Jimmy Sr told her.

—That's nice.

—We'll be wantin' sequins on our jerseys, isn't tha' righ', Darren?

—No way. ——Oh yeah! Yeah.

Darren gasped, keeping the laugh in. Jimmy Sr nudged Darren. Darren nudged Jimmy Sr. Snot burst out of Darren's nose because he was trying not to laugh, but Jimmy Sr didn't mind. His cardigan was due a wash anyway.

Veronica flicked through the channels while the ads were on.

—How's this for a name, Darren? ——The Barrytown Wheelies.

—Brilliant!

Darren couldn't stay sitting any more.

—Better than the oul' Barrytown Cyclin' Club, wha'.

—Ah yeah!

—I'll tell yeh wha'. Go an' see if yeh can get a few o' your chums to join. All o' them. The more the merrier. We'll poach them.

He laughed.

—That'll teach the bollix.

Darren dashed to the door.

—You'll never keep it up, said Veronica.

—Won't I? said Jimmy Sr. —Who says I won't? I'm serious abou' this, yeh know. I've been doin' a lot o' thinkin' these days an', well ——I'm his father an' —

Darren jumped back in.

—Da.

—Yes, Darren?

—Can girls be in the club?

Jimmy Sr looked at Darren. He wanted to give him the right answer. He guessed.

—Yeah ——probably.

—Rapid! Thanks.

Darren was gone again. Jimmy Sr turned back to Veronica.

—That's mah boy, he said.

—Are you crying?

—No, I amn't! ——Jaysis! ——It's the smoke.

—What smoke?

—Fuck off an' stop annoyin' me.

*   *   *

Sharon was passing her before she saw her. She'd been too busy thinking about wanting to get out; she felt really squashed in and surrounded and sticky. Then she saw her and before she had time even to say, Jesus, it's her, she said —Hiyeh, Yvonne.

Yvonne Burgess saw who it was. She turned back quickly and continued to flick through the rack of skirts.

Sharon stayed for a second, half deciding to force Yvonne to talk to her.

Yvonne spoke.

—Terrible smell in here, isn't there, Mary?

Sharon then saw that Mary Curran —she hadn't seen her in months —was on the other side of the rack. She wasn't exactly hiding but that was what she was doing all the same.

Mary didn't say anything.

Sharon stood there a bit more, then went on.

She heard Yvonne again, louder.

—They shouldn't let prostitutes in here, sure they shouldn't, Mary?

Sharon grinned.

God help her, she thought. She couldn't blame her really. At least she hadn't tried to beat her up or anything. That Mary one was a right cow though, pretending she hadn't seen her.

Spotty bitch. Even Mister Burgess wouldn't have gone near her.

* * *

—What's tha' shite? said Jimmy Sr. —What's tha' under the hedge there? ——A hedgehog, is it? The head on it, wha'.

—It's David Attenborough.

—It looks like a hedgehog, said Jimmy Sr.

They laughed.

—It's abou' hedgehogs, said Sharon. —Wildlife On One.

—Ah yeah. Jaysis, look at him! The speed of him. Where's the remote till we hear wha' David's sayin'.

—Oh look it, said Sharon. —There's two o' them now.

Jimmy Jr came in.

—Typical, said Jimmy Sr. —Walkin' in just when the nookie's startin'.

Jimmy Jr sat down, on the other side of Sharon.

—What's thot? he said.

—A hudgehog, said Jimmy Sr. —Two hudgehogs. Roidin'.

—Fuck off.

—Keep your feet up there, Sharon, said Jimmy Sr.
—You'll get cramps.

—I'm goin' to the toilet.

—Oh, fair enough. ——So that's how they do it. That's very clever all the same. Off he goes again, look it. Back into the hedge. Didn't even say goodbye or thanks or ann'thin'. That's nature for yeh.

Jimmy Jr was bored. He didn't like nature programmes or things like that. But he wanted to talk to Sharon so he stayed where he was.

Jimmy Sr sniffed.

—Are you wearin' perfume?

—Fuck off.

Sharon came back and sat between the Jimmys.

—Feet up, Sharon, said Jimmy Sr. —That's righ'.

—Come here, said Jimmy Jr.

But Jimmy Sr got to her first.

—Only a few more weeks to go now, wha'.

—Yeah, said Sharon.

—Sharon, said Jimmy Jr.

—Wha'?

—Do us a favour, will yeh.

—I was just lookin' at your, eh, stomach there, Jimmy Sr told Sharon. —It's movin' all over the place.

—Wha'? Sharon asked Jimmy Jr.

—I can't tell yeh here —

—Do you mind! said Jimmy Sr.

—Wha'? said Jimmy Jr.

—I was talkin' to Sharon.

Jimmy Jr leaned out so he could see past Sharon.

—So?

—So fuck off. Go upstairs an' spin your discs.

Sharon was laughing.

Jimmy Sr was looking at his watch. He stood up.

—You've got three minutes, he said. —I'll check an' see if Veronica's fixed Darren's jersey yet.

—Did he crash again?

—No. The fuckin' dog was swingin' off it when it was on the line.

He was gone. Jimmy Jr stood up and shut the door.

—I've a gig in a few weeks; Soturday, he told Sharon.

—Stop talkin' like tha', will yeh.

——I'm tryin' to get used to it.

—It makes yeh sound like a fuckin' eejit.

—Here maybe, but not on the radio, said Jimmy.

—Anywhere, said Sharon.

—The lessons cost me forty fuckin' quid, said Jimmy.

—You were robbed, said Sharon. —Yeh sound like a dope. ——Roight?

—Fuck up a minute. I've a gig on, Soh-Saturday fortnight.

—Wha' gig?

—On the radio, said Jimmy.

She looked as if she didn't believe him.

—The community radio. You know. ——Andy Dudley's garage.

—Tha'!

—Yeah; tha'!

Sharon roared.

—Don't start, said Jimmy. —Wacker Mulcahy —he calls himself Lee Bradley on Saturdays —he has to do best man at his brother's weddin'. So Andy said I can have his slot.

—His wha'?

—His slot.

—That's disgustin'.

—Oh yeah.

They both laughed.

—Annyway, listen.

He switched on his new accent.

—Hoy there, you there, out there. This is Jommy Robbitte, Thot's Rockin' Robbitte, with a big fot hour of the
meanest, hottest, baddest sounds arouuund; yeahhh.
——How's tha'?

—Thick.

—Fuckin' thanks.

—No, it's good. Rockin' Rabbitte, I like tha'.

—Do yeh? ——I was thinkin' o' callin' meself Gary
——eh, Gary Breeze.

Sharon had a hankie in her sleeve and she got it to her
nose just in time.

—I'll stick to Rockin' Rabbitte, will I? said Jimmy.

He grinned. Sharon nodded.

—Yeah.

Jimmy Sr was back.

—Hop it.

—Righ'. Thanks, Sharon.

Jimmy Jr left.

—Was he annoyin' yeh? said Jimmy Sr.

—Ah no.

—You've enough on your plate withou' that eejit hasslin'
yeh. ——Righ'. Annyway, Sharon, what I wanted to say
was: how're yeh feelin'?

—Grand.

—You're not nervous or worried or ann'thin'?

—No, she lied. —Not really.

—Three weeks.

—Twenty days.

—That's righ'. ——I've been thinkin' a bit, said Jimmy
Sr. —An', well; if yeh want I'll —

The twins charged in, just like the cavalry.

—Daddy, said Linda. —Mister Reeves says you're to
hurry up an' he says if we get you ou' of the house in a
minute he'll give us a pound.

Jimmy Sr patted Sharon's leg.

—I'll get back to yeh abou' tha', he said.

—Okay, said Sharon.

About what? she wondered.

—Righ', girls, said Jimmy Sr. —Let's get this pound off o' Bimbo.

That left Sharon alone. She laughed a bit, then closed her eyes.

* * *

She didn't wait at her usual bus-stop, across from work. She kept going, around the corner to the stop with the shelter. There was no one else there.

She couldn't stop crying. She wasn't trying to stop.

She leaned her back against the shelter ad. She gulped, and let herself slide down to the ground. She fell the last bit. She didn't know how she'd get up again. She didn't care.

She gulped, and gulped, and cried.

* * *

Sharon tried to explain it to Veronica.

—I'm sick of it, she said.

She tried harder.

—I hate it, watchin' the oul' ones countin' their twopences out o' their purses an' lookin' at yeh as if you were goin' to rob them. An' listenin' to them complainin' abou' the weather an' the prices o' things.

Her mother was still looking hard.

—And anyway, said Sharon. —Me back's really killin' me these days an' I'm always wantin' to go to the toilet an' —

She was crying.

—tha' bastard Moloney is always houndin' me. He's only

a shelf stacker in a suit, an' Gerry Dempsey —prick! —he put his arm round me. In front of everyone, an' he said to give him a shout if I was havin' anny more babies. ——An' I'm sick of it an' I'm not goin' back. I don't care!

Veronica wanted to go around to Sharon and hold her but —

—Sharon, love, she said. —A job's a job. Could you not wait —

—I don't care, I'm not goin'. You can't make me.

Veronica let it go.

—You'd love to make me go back, wouldn't yeh? said Sharon. —Well, I'm not goin' to. I don't care. ——All you care abou' is the money.

Veronica got out of the kitchen. She sat on the bed in her room.

* * *

—Yeh did righ', Sharon, said Jimmy Sr.

—Yeah ——well —

—No; you were dead righ'.

—It was just —Sharon started; then stopped.

—I shouldn't have paid any attention to them, she said. —I'd only the rest of the week to go anyway. I'll go back tomorrow an' —

—You won't, said Jimmy Sr. —If yeh don't want to.

—Sure, me maternity leave; I've three months off after Saturday annyway.

—Well, you've the rest o' your life off if yeh want it, wha'.

—Wha' abou' Mammy?

—Your mammy's grand, said Jimmy Sr. —She doesn't want you to go back there if you don't want to either. She was just a bit worried abou' you havin' no job after you have the baby ——but —She's grand. She doesn't want you to go in an' be treated like tha' ——by thicks.

—Ah —said Sharon.

She'd been thinking about it.

—They ARE fuckin' thick, she said. —If he'd said it —half an hour earlier even I'd've told him to feck off or I'd've laughed or —But when he said it ——an' they all started laughin', I just —If he said it now ——

—We'd feed the bits of him to the dog, wha'.

—Yeah.

—You're not goin' back so.

It was sort of a question.

—No.

—Good.

—I'd like to go back just ——An' walk ou' properly, yeh know?

—I do, yeah. ——The lady o' leisure, wha'.

—Yeah.

—Wish I was.

* * *

—Ah fuck this, said Jimmy Sr.

He let go of the lawn-mower. He looked at his palms. He was sure he'd ripped the skin off them. But, no, it was still there, and bit redder but alright. That meant he'd have to keep going.

—Fuck it, he said.

Jimmy Sr was cutting the grass, the front. Last night Bimbo had called Jimmy Sr's house Vietnam because of the state of the front garden. Jimmy Sr had laughed. But when Bimbo told him that everyone called it that Jimmy Sr'd said, Enough; fuck it, he'd cut the grass tomorrow, the cunts.

—Give us a lend o' your lawn-mower, Bimbo, he'd said.

—No way, Bimbo'd said.

—Ah go on, he'd said, —for fuck sake. I'll give it back to yeh this time.

—Okay, Bimbo'd said.

—Good man, he'd said.

So here he was trying to cut the grass. In November.

—Fuck Bimbo, he said to himself.

The grass was too long for the mower. And it was damp, so the mower kept skidding. He'd have to get the shears to it first. Bimbo'd insisted that he take the shears as well when he'd called for the mower. That was why he said Fuck Bimbo.

He'd have to get down on his hunkers now. But it had to be done.

He was a changed man, a new man. That trouble a while back with Sharon had given him an awful fright and, more important, it had made him feel like a right useless oul' bollix. He'd done a lot of thinking since then. And a lot of reading, and looking at pictures. Those little foetuses all curled up ——with their fingers, and the lot.

There was more to life than drinking pints with your mates. There was Veronica, his wife, and his children. Some of his own sperms had gone into making them so, fuck it, he was responsible for them. But, my Jaysis, he'd made one poxy job of it so far. Bimbo'd said he was being too hard on himself; his kids were grand, but Jimmy Sr'd said that that was just good luck and Veronica because he'd had nothing to do with it. But from now on it was going to be different. Darren and Linda and Tracy, and even Leslie, were still young enough, and then there'd be Sharon's little snapper as well. A strong active man in the house, a father figure, would be vital for Sharon's snapper.

—Vital, Bimbo. Vital.

—Oh God, yes, Bimbo'd agreed.

So cutting the grass was important. The new short grass

would be a sort of announcement: there's a new man living in this house, so fuck off and mind your own business.

Jimmy Sr looked at the garden. For a small garden it grew a terrible lot of grass. The Corporation should have cut it; he'd always said it. But they were useless.

It was up to him.

He chose a spot to put his knees. It looked soft.

There was a problem but. Any minute now Darren would come flying around the corner, down the road and past the house and he'd be expecting Jimmy Sr to shout out how long the lap had taken him. Because, as well as cutting the grass, Jimmy Sr was training the Barrytown Wheelies Under 14 squad; Darren and three of his pals. They had a team time trial at the weekend and Darren had said that they'd have to be ready and Jimmy Sr agreed with him. So he had them doing laps of the estate, and he was pretending to time them. He was only pretending because he couldn't get the hang of the stop-watch Bertie'd got him. He couldn't admit this to the team because it would've been bad for morale. The last thing a new, breakaway, very keen team needed to know was that their manager couldn't operate the stop-watch.

He'd wait till they cycled past, then he'd do a few minutes shearing and he'd be waiting for them when they came around again.

He leaned on the wall and held the stop-watch ready. It looked like an easy enough yoke to use. He was sure it was. He'd bring it up to the Hikers and see if one of the lads could figure it out.

—How's it goin', Mister Rabbitte?

Jimmy Sr looked. It was one of Jimmy Jr's pals, Mickah Wallace.

—Howyeh, Mick, said Jimmy Sr. —He's upstairs doin' his DJin'. Or shavin' his legs or somethin'. No fear of him givin' me a hand here an' annyway, that's for fuckin' certain.

—Wha'; holdin' the wall up?

—Wha' ——No. No; I'm cuttin' the grass. Hang on, here they come.

Darren was first. He came out of Chestnut Drive onto Chestnut Avenue. He was slowing but he still had to go up on the far path to get a wide enough angle to turn. Then he was through two parked cars, back onto the road and across to the proper side and towards Jimmy Sr and Mickah, picking up speed again. Two more followed Darren across the road, onto the path. One of them got too close to the wall and must have scraped his knee. The last lad was on an ordinary bike, the poor little sap. No gears or nothing. Jimmy Sr would've loved to have got him a proper bike, if he'd had the money. But he didn't have it. And anyway, he was the manager. He had to be ruthless. If he didn't have gears he'd just have to pedal faster. He was part of a team.

Darren raced past him. Jimmy Sr stared at the stopwatch. He pressed one of the black twirly knobs at the top.

He roared.

—Thirteen seconds faster! Good man, Darren!

But Darren was gone.

—Thirteen seconds up, lads! Good lads!

Mickah admired their yellow jerseys. They had The Hiker's Rest —Pub Grub printed across the backs.

The last one, Eric Rickard, was suffering.

—Come on, Paddy Last, Jimmy Sr roared as Eric came up to them. —Catch up with him. Come on.

His face was white. His legs weren't really long enough for the bike. He had to shift from side to side as he pedalled. The bollix must've been torn off him.

But he was pedalling away like bejaysis.

—Good lad, good man, good man. ——Poor little fucker.

Mickah was laughing. He'd enjoyed all that.

—The hurlin' helmets look deadly, he said.

—Yeah, said Jimmy Sr. —Your man, the Hikers' manager, bought them for us as well. One for me even as well.

—Fair play. Jimmy's inside an' anyway?

—Yeah. Spinnin' the discs.

Jimmy Sr looked down at the grass.

—Fuckin' hell.

He was bending his knees experimentally.

—Wish I was younger.

Mickah was still there.

—A good bit younger, said Mickah.

—Fuck off, you, said Jimmy Sr. —He's up in his room. Go on ahead in.

Jimmy Sr got down on his knees.

—Oh, bollix to it.

Mickah stood there with his hands in his pockets, his head tilted a bit to one side.

—Wha'? said Jimmy Sr.

—Just lookin'.

—Are you actin' the prick?

—No! No; it's just I've never seen yeh doin' annythin' before, yeh know. Can I watch?

—Fuck off ou' o' tha'. It's hard enough without havin' bollixes like you gawkin' at —

—Watch ou'!

Darren was coming.

Jimmy Sr got up and ran to the wall.

—Seven seconds down, Darren! Seven seconds! Come on now. —Come on, lads; yis're laggin' behind. Nine seconds down. Come on now. Good lads. One last drive. Come on.

There was no sign of Eric. Jimmy Sr turned back to Mickah.

—Tha' was close.

Mickah ran around Jimmy Sr and ducked in behind the

wall. Jimmy Sr looked around, and saw George Burgess coming down his path to the gate.

Then Mickah started singing.

—OH ——TIE A YELLOW RIBBON —

ROUND THE OLD OAK TREE —

George looked over at Jimmy Sr.

—Don't look at me, Burgess!

—IT'S BEEN THREE LONG YEARS —

DO YEH STILL WANT ME —

DA RAH DA RAH—

Jimmy Sr held up the shears.

—Yeh know wha' I'd like to do with these, Burgess, don't yeh?

—Go on, Mister Rabbitte, said Mickah, still crouched behind the wall. —Have him ou'. Go on. I'll back yeh up.

Eric cycled by.

—Good man, Eric! Good man, son. One more now, one more, then we'll call it a day. Good lad. ——Hope he doesn't die on us.

George kept walking. He didn't look back. Mickah stood up. They both looked at George walking down Chestnut Avenue.

—You SHOULD knock the shite ou' of him though, Mickah told Jimmy Sr.

—Why? said Jimmy Sr. —He didn't do annythin' to me.

Mickah thought about this. He studied Jimmy Sr carefully.

—Maybe he didn't, he said. —But yeh should still give him a hidin'.

—Why?

—Cos you'd beat him.

Jimmy Sr got down on his knees at the edge of the grass.

—That's why I couldn't be bothered, he said. —Jaysis, look it!

—Wha'?

Jimmy Sr held up a well mauled and weathered ten pound note.

—Nice one, said Mickah.

—It was in the grass, said Jimmy Sr. —Just there. That's gas.

He stood up.

—What're yeh goin' to do with it? Mickah asked him.

—Well, said Jimmy Sr. —I'm goin' to give five of it to Leslie. After he's cut this fuckin' grass.

—Good thinkin', said Mickah.

—An' maybe a nice set o' handlebars for poor Eric.

—Ah, said Mickah. —Nice one.

* * *

Sharon got Linda to open the window a bit before she went down for her breakfast. Now she was alone in the bedroom. She sat up against all the pillows, and listened. The room was at the back of the house but she could still hear enough. She'd heard about five cars starting, including her daddy's —it always coughed before it got going. She could hear kids shouting, going into the school. She heard a front door slamming, and back ones —the sound was different. But best of all was the clicking of heels. That meant girls dashing to work, and she wasn't one of them.

It was brilliant. She'd been doing this every morning since she'd given up work.

She didn't care much about the money. The pay had been useless anyway. She'd be getting her allowance after the baby was born and her daddy was going to give her some money every week, once he'd sorted it out with her mammy. She'd only have to stay in the house a bit more often and she'd be doing that anyway because of the baby. So it was great.

Her back wasn't hurting her that much. The baby's head

had settled and sometimes it felt like she wasn't pregnant any more. But never for long. She was dry and clean. She was nice and tired. She wanted to go to the toilet but not enough yet to get up. She was going to read a bit of her book, Lace II —it was a bit thick but she liked it and she liked being able to get through the pages fast. Then she'd go down and have her breakfast. She'd see if she could get her mammy to come out for a walk or something. She'd watch a bit of telly as well; there'd be videos on Sky and Super.

She couldn't make her mind up about the name. Fiona or Lorraine; she liked them. Mark, if it was a boy. Or maybe James. Her daddy would love that. But then he might take over the baby, the way he was these days. And there'd be three Jimmys in the house. She didn't know.

It had gone quiet outside. There were no cars. Everyone was gone.

Her belly button was like a real button now; inside out. She didn't like it that way. It felt dangerous.

She heard something; someone was running and wheezing, and the steps weren't very fast. The wheezing must have been really bad if she could hear it from the back of the house. And now it was raining again. She hoped it was Mister Burgess out there. Not really though.

It was nice.

But she still couldn't stop worrying. It could happen any time. She was having these —painless contractions the book called them —all the time, now and again, but they weren't really painless at all because they made her really nervous because the next one might be painful, and she waited and waited for the next one until she ached.

She got up. She wanted to be in the kitchen.

* * *

—Oh Jesus! said Sharon.

—What's wrong? said Jimmy Sr.

He jumped up off the couch.

—Is it comin', is it?

—No, said Sharon.

She shifted, to get the cushions behind her again.

—Sorry. I was just fallin' asleep an' I didn't know it, em —Sorry.

Jimmy Sr looked disappointed. He sat down, but he was ready to get up again.

—Yeh can't be too careful abou' this sort o' thing, he said.

Veronica climbed out of the armchair and stood up.

—We don't want you bursting your waters all over the furniture, isn't that right, Jimmy dear? They're new covers.

She went out, into the kitchen.

Jimmy Sr sat there, appalled. That was the dirtiest, foulest thing he'd heard in his life. And his wife had said it!

Sharon was laughing.

—Jaysis, Sharon, I'm sorry, said Jimmy Sr. —Tha' was a terrible thing for Veronica to say. Terrible.

—Ah, stop it, said Sharon. —She was only jokin.

—No, no, said Jimmy Sr. —There's jokin' an' jokin' but tha' was no fuckin' joke. I'm just glad the twins weren't here to hear it.

—Ah Daddy!

—No, Sharon, Jimmy Sr insisted. —This is no laughin' matter.

He pointed at Sharon's belly.

—Do yeh not realize tha' there's a livin' bein' in there? he said. —A livin' ——thing.

—Ah, feck off, Daddy. Cop on.

—Don't start tha' raisin' your eyes to heaven shite with me. An' don't start chewin' tha' fuckin' celery when I'm talkin' to yeh.

Sharon tapped Jimmy Sr on the head with her celery.

—Yes, Daddy.

She gulped.

—The livin' bein' in here is givin' me terrible fuckin' indigestion, she said.

—That's cos your stomach's flattened, Jimmy Sr told her. —Yeh prob'ly ate too much.

—I didn't.

—Yeh should only eat small amounts.

—Ah, shag off.

—It looks like there's only one person takin' this thing seriously, an' that's me.

—Excuse me! said Sharon. —I am takin' it seriously. I'm the one carryin' it around with me all the time.

—You're gettin' snotty now cos o' your hormones, Jimmy Sr told her. —I'll talk to yeh later.

Sharon laughed at this.

—There's nothin' wrong with my hormones.

—I didn't say there was annythin' wrong with them, said Jimmy Sr. —No, there's nothin' wrong. As such. Wrong's the wrong word. Imbalance is the term I'd use.

—Thanks very much, Doctor Rabbitte.

—Fuck off.

Then he grinned. Then he stopped grinning, and coughed.

—When, he said. —When your mammy ——Times have changed, d'yeh know tha'?

Sharon smiled.

—When your mammy was havin' Jimmy I was in work. An' when she was havin' you I was in me mother's. When she had Leslie I was inside in town, in Conways, yeh know, with the lads. The Hikers wasn't built then. For Darren, I was —I can't remember. The twins, I was in the Hikers.

—You've a great memory.

—Nowadays the husbands are there with the women, said Jimmy Sr. —That's much better, I think. I'd ——

He scratched his leg.

—Because he can hold her hand an' help her, an' encourage her, yeh know, an' see his child bein' born.

There wasn't even a car going past. The pipes upstairs weren't making any noise.

—Sharon, I'll —Only if yeh want now ——I wouldn't mind stayin' with you when ——you're havin' it.

—Ah no.

——Okay.

* * *

—Stop pushin' her, will yeh!

Sharon and Jackie were in Howth, on stools at the bar. It was busy and getting busier.

—I'm tryin' to get tha' prick of a barman to serve me, said the young fella in the black polo neck and glowing dandruff who'd pushed Sharon's back. He was wedged between Sharon and one of the poles that held up the ceiling, on his toes and clicking his fingers.

—Look at her condition, will yeh, said Jackie.

He did, still clicking his fingers.

—She doesn't look tha' bad, he said.

—She's pregnant, yeh fuckin' sap.

—Fuck, sorry!

—Yeah; so yeh should be. ——I'll get the barman for yeh. Raymond!

Raymond was there before she'd finished calling him.

—Yeah?

—He wants yeh.

—Oh. ——Yeah?

—He fancies yeh, said Sharon.

—I know, said Jackie. —He nearly dribbles all over me. Did yeh see him there? His fuckin' tongue was hangin' ou'.

She copied Raymond.

—Yeah? Yeah? Yeah?

Sharon laughed.

—Ah stop. He's not tha' bad.

—I suppose he isn't. He's still a spa though.

Sharon laughed again.

—You're a terrible fuckin' wagon, Jackie. ——I'm pissed.

—So am I, said Jackie. —Raymond!

—Yeah?

—Same again, chicken.

—Yeah.

He ran over to the optics.

—Yeah, said Jackie.

She lifted herself up a bit so she could see all of Raymond.

—He's got a nice arse on him all the same.

She sat down again.

—Pity abou' the rest of him.

—I'm pissed, Jackie, said Sharon.

—So am I, said Jackie.

Sharon looked down.

—I shouldn't be doin' this.

—Wha'?

—Drinkin'.

—Ah, don't be thick, Sharon. Yeh need to get pissed now
an' again. There's no harm in it.

—Yeah, said Sharon.

She tried to sit up.

—Thank you, Raymond, said Jackie. —You're the best
little barman in the world.

—An' the best lookin', said Sharon.

—Oh def'ny, said Jackie.

Raymond grinned and blushed and dropped tenpence
into Jackie's glass, and decided not to try and get it out
after he'd already put two of his fingers into the vodka.

—I want another one, said Jackie. —I'm not takin' tha'.

—Okay, said Raymond. —Sorry abou' tha'.

He went over to the optics, got the tenpence out, filled a new glass, but left it on the counter and brought Jackie back her old one.

—There, he said.

—Thank you, Raymond. I'll have my change now. If you don't mind.

—Oh yeah.

Sharon couldn't stop laughing. Her hand shook when she poured the Coke in on top of the vodka.

—Thank you very much, Raymond, said Jackie when Raymond came back with the tenpence. —Better late than never.

Sharon pushed the tears off her nose.

—Is me mascara alrigh'? she asked.

—Ah yeah, said Jackie. —Yeh'd want to be lookin'.

—Me back's fuckin' killin' me. We shouldn't've sitten here. I need somethin' to lean against.

—The pole, said Jackie.

—Yeah, said Sharon.

She came down off her stool.

—Jesus! ——God, I'm pissed, d'yeh know tha'.

She straightened up.

—Jesus.

She picked up the stool.

—'Xcuse me. Out o' me way.

She shoved the stool between the bar and a man who was waiting at it, and reached the pole. Jackie followed her. They got back onto the stools. Sharon leaned back. The pole was cold through her clothes.

—That's lovely.

—What're YOU lookin' at? Jackie asked a spotty young fella.

—Nothin'!

—Better not be. ——Where's me drink? Jesus, I'm finished already.

—My turn, said Sharon.

She knocked back the rest of hers.

—You call him, okay? she said to Jackie.

—Raymond!

—Same again?

—Yeah, said Jackie. —Yeah.

—Oh fuh-fuck, said Sharon. —I've got the hic-coughs.

She put her hand on her chest, to feel for any approaching hiccups.

—Jesus, I'm scuttered. ——They're gone.

—Wha'?

—The hi-hi —Fuck it, they're back.

There was a new song on the jukebox.

—Oh, I love this one, said Jackie.

—Yeah, said Sharon. —He's a ride, isn't he?

—He is, yeah, said Jackie. —A riyed! I'd love to dig me nails —

—Talkin' abou' rides, lo-look who's behind yeh, Jackie. Don't turn.

But she'd turned already.

—Where?

—There.

—Where!

—There. Look it, yeh blind bitch. Beside your woman.

—Who is it? ——Oh Jesus Christ!

It was Greg, Jackie's ex, the fella she'd blown out in the ILAC Centre because the cream in his eclair had gone missing.

Jackie turned back and faced the bar.

—Is he lookin' this way?

—Yeah, said Sharon. —He's seen yeh. Oh Jesus, he's comin' over, Jackie.

—I won't talk to him, I don't care. I fuckin' won't.

—He's takin' somethin' ou' of his trousers. Oh my God, Jackie!

Jackie had copped on by now. She turned and saw the back of Greg's head way over on the other side of the lounge.

—You're a fuckin' cunt, Rabbitte.

She hoped she hadn't sounded too disappointed. She laughed with Sharon, just in case.

—I think I'm goin' to be sick, said Sharon.

Her face was really white.

—Oh Jesus, said Jackie. —Come on.

She slid off her stool.

Sharon shook her head.

—I won't make it.

She grabbed her bag from the counter. She unclasped and opened it quickly. It wasn't a big bag but she got as much of her head as she could into it; her chin, her mouth and her nose. Then she puked. It was a quick rush of vodka and Coke and a few little things. Then up with her head and she shut the bag.

Jackie gave her a paper hankie. She wiped her mouth and opened the bag a bit and threw the tissue in on top of the vodka and the rest. She held the bag up.

—It should hold, she said. —I'll bring it ou' and empty it in a minute.

They both laughed. Sharon felt much better already. She gave herself a test burp: grand; there was no taste off it or anything.

—Did annyone see me? she said.

—Yeah, said Jackie. —I think so. Your man there, look. He was lookin' at yeh.

—Him? Specky Features? I wouldn't mind him.

—You were very fast, said Jackie.

—There wasn't tha' much, said Sharon.

They drank to it. The vodka put up no fight going down. Sharon relaxed. She dropped the bag onto the floor.

—Squelch, said Jackie.

—I'm fuckin' pissed.

—Hiyis.

Mary Curran was standing between them.

—Mary! said Jackie. —Howyeh.

—Hiyis, said Mary. —Haven't seen yis in ages.

—Yeh saw me a few weeks ago, said Sharon.

—When, Sharon?

—You know fuckin' well when, Mary. In Dunnes with Yvonne.

—I didn't see yeh, Sharon.

—Yeh did so.

—I didn't Sharon; when?

—Ah, who cares when? said Jackie. —Yeh see each other now, don't yis?

—Yeah ——Well —

—Jesus, Sharon, sorry.

—Yeah. ——Sorry for shoutin' at yeh.

—Your hair's lovely, Mary, said Jackie.

—Yeah, said Sharon.

—Thanks. How are yeh, Sharon, an' annyway?

—Alrigh', said Sharon. —Grand.

—She's pissed, said Jackie.

—Fuck off, you. I am not.

—You look fabulous, Mary told Sharon.

—Thanks.

—When're yeh due?

—Monday.

—Jesus, that's brilliant.

—But it'll be late prob'ly.

—Yeh must be thrilled, are yeh?

—Ah yeah.

They were struggling, but they tried.

—Who're yeh with, Mary? said Sharon.

—A fella.

—Who?

—You know him, Jackie. Greg.

Sharon looked at Jackie.

—Does he still like eclairs? said Jackie.

—Pardon?

—Nothin'. Tell him I was askin' for him, will yeh.

—Yeah. ——I'd better go back.

—Yeah. See yeh, Mary.

—See yeh, Jackie. See yeh, Sharon. I'll come in to see yeh when you're in the hospital.

—Thanks. See yeh.

—See yeh, Mary. Bye bye. ——Yeh fuckin' cow yeh. She's a titless bitch, isn't she?

They laughed.

—I never liked her, said Jackie.

—Jesus, I'm pissed.

—My turn, said Jackie. —Raymond!

—Yeah? Same again?

—S'il vous plait.

—Yeah.

—Yeah. ——Wha' did yeh think of her fuckin' hair?

Sharon slid off the stool, and nearly fell.

—I'm goin' home, she said.

—Are yeh alrigh'?

—Yeah, I think —I'd better go home.

Jackie picked up their bags.

—Come on, she said.

* * *

She was afraid to close her eyes. She didn't want to get sick again. She was glad she was home. She wouldn't go out again, even if the baby was weeks late.

Even in the taxi, before it moved even, she knew that nothing was going to happen. But she didn't tell Jackie that. She just wanted to get home. She'd sort of panicked;

thought she'd felt something, a real contraction or something, and the heat and the smoke and the crowds got to
her and she had to get out of the pub and come home.
She'd been sick twice since she got home but she wasn't
going to be again. As well as that though, she'd wanted to
go to the toilet really badly, like she had the runs, but she
hadn't gone nearly as much as she thought she'd needed to
but she still felt like she wanted to go, and that was
supposed to be a sign that the labour would be starting
soon, so it was just as well that she was here at home.

Could it start when you were asleep? she wondered.
She'd wake up. Wouldn't she? Anyway, she didn't think
she'd be able to sleep. She was terrified.

She'd felt better the minute she got into the taxi. The
driver had been nice, telling them he was going to charge
them for three because of the size of Sharon. And Jackie
told him to hurry up or he'd be charging for three alright,
and paying for the cleaning. It'd been nice. And then when
Sharon opened her bag to pay him!

She wished she'd someone to talk to.

It was going to hurt. Jesus, it was like waiting to be
stabbed, knowing for definite you were going to be, but not
when, only soon. It wasn't fair. It was cruel. She'd never do
this to anyone.

*   *   *

—They're a bit smelly, Jimmy Sr admitted. —But they're
not too bad.

He threw the jerseys on the floor.

—Are yeh alrigh', Sharon?

—Yeah.

—Sure?

—Yeah!

—Are yeh constipated at all?

—Lay off, Daddy, will yeh.

—Fair enough. I was only askin'.

—Well, don't.

——Tea, said Jimmy Sr.

He went over to the kettle and looked at it.

—You get the water from the tap, said Veronica, who'd just come in.

—Ha ha, said Jimmy Sr.

He put the kettle under the tap, and sang.

—OH YEH-HESS —

I'M THE GREAT PRE-TE-HENDER —

DO DOO —DO DOO —DO —

The twins came barging in the back door. They had their dancing dresses on under their anoraks.

—There's the girls, said Jimmy Sr. —How 'd yis get on, girls?

—We didn't come last, Tracy told them.

—Course yeh didn't, said Jimmy Sr. —We didn't either. Darren, eh, acquitted himself very well. An' buckled his wheel.

—Teresa Kelly's shoe broke an' she fell, said Linda.

—Yeah, said Tracy. —An' she said somethin' rude an' they disqualified her.

—Yeah, an' her ma dragged her —

—Mammy!

—Her mammy dragged her ou' an' yeh could hear her dress rippin'.

Jimmy Sr laughed. He switched the kettle on.

—There. ——Poor Teresa.

—We hate her, said Linda.

—Course yeh do, said Jimmy Sr. —When's the big one? Next week, is it?

—Yeah.

—We'll all have to go to tha'.

—You're not to, said Linda. —Only if yeh want to.

—You can hold our coats an' our handbags, said Tracy.

—Thanks very much, said Jimmy Sr.

—What handbags? said Veronica.

—Missis McPartland says we've to have —

—No!

—Ah now, Veronica, said Jimmy Sr. —Maybe Santy'll come a bit early.

—Ah, no way, said Linda. —I don't want a handbag from Santy.

—We'll see wha' happens.

Sharon had gone upstairs for her radio. She had it ready.

—Listen, she said.

She turned it on. Alexander O'Neal was singing Fake.

—Wha'? said Jimmy Sr.

—Shut up an' listen a minute, said Sharon.

Fake was ending. Then they heard him.

—THOT WAS OLEXONDER O'NEAL WITH FAKE. THERE'S NOTHIN' FAKE ABOUT THIS ONE. HERE'S THE GODFATHER OF SOUL. ——JAMES BROWN, YIS SIMPLEHEADS YIS.

James Brown sang Living in America. Sharon turned it down.

—Was tha' Jimmy? said Jimmy Sr.

—Yeah, said Sharon.

—Was it, Sharon? said Tracy.

—Yeah.

—Janey.

—Jimmy on the radio.

—Wha' station is it? Jimmy Sr asked.

—Radio 2, Sharon lied.

—Go 'way. Jimmy?

—Yeah. He's fillin' in for someone on their holidays.

—Go 'way. ——Jimmy, wha'. Turn it up.

He listened to James Brown.

—We're some family all the same, wha'.

He smiled at Veronica, and nodded at the radio.

—Cyclin', ——dancin', DJin on the radio. Havin' babies. ——Y'alrigh', Sharon?

—Yeah ——

She looked shocked, and scared.

——I think I'm startin'.

—Sure?

—Yeah. ——Yeah.

—Up yeh go, girls, an' get Sharon's bag for her, said Jimmy Sr.

—Are yeh havin' the baby, Sharon?

—Get up!

—And —Ah! —an' me toothbrush, Tracy.

—ROIGHT. ROCKIN' ROBBITTE COMIN' AT YOUUU, FILLIN' IN FOR LEE BRADLEY. HOW'S YOUR WEEKEND GOIN'? ——TOUGH.

—We're some family alrigh', said Jimmy Sr.

He grinned at Sharon.

—Come on, Sharon.

—THIS ONE'S FOR ANTO AN' GILLIAN WHO WERE SNARED BEHIND THE CLINIC LAST NIGHT BY FATHER MOLLOY. YEOW, ANTO!

Jimmy Sr was out starting the car, so he didn't hear that bit.

* * *

—The lights are turnin' green for us, look it, said Jimmy Sr.

—Yeah.

—That's the second one. Must be a good sign, wha'.

—Yeah.

—Soon be over.

—Yeah.

—Don't worry, love. ——God, wait'll yeh have it in your arms, wha'. Jaysis, women have all the luck. ——Y'alrigh'?

—Yeah.

—Good girl. Don't hold the handle so tight there, Sharon. You might fall ou'.

—Sorry.

—No problem. ——Shite; they've turned red up here. Can't expect them all to be green, I suppose.

He slowed the car, then gripped Sharon's hand.

—Good girl. It's only the oul' cervix dilatin'. ——It could happen to a bishop, wha'.

He got the car going again.

—Here, Sharon. Look it; here's me watch. Yeh can time the contractions so you'll be able to tell them when we get there. They'll be impressed. ——Oh, God help yeh. Sit back, Sharon, good girl. Take deep breaths, good girl. Good deep breaths. That's wha' I always do, wha'.

He was going to turn on the radio.

—Let's listen to Jimmy.

—He'd be over by now.

—Ah well. He was very good, wasn't he? ——Did yeh time tha' one, Sharon?

—Ye-yeah. ——Thirty-seven seconds, ——abou'.

—That's grand, said Jimmy Sr. —Nearly there now. Summerhill, look it. Straight down now an' we're there. Green again up here, look it.

—Yeah.

—That's great. Is it God or the Corporation, would yeh say?

————

—Tha' place has changed its name again, look it. ——Good girl, sit back. Good girl. Deep breaths. ——Get ou' of me way, yeh fuckin' ——! Gobshite; I should have run over him. The thick head on him, did yeh see it? Good girl. ——Here we are, Sharon, look.

* * *

The nurse, the nice one, wiped Sharon's face.

—Th-thanks. ——Will it hurt anny more?

—Not really, love. We're nearly there now.

—How long more —

—Quiet, Sharon. Come on; breathe with me. ——In ——

The breath became a gasp and a scream as Sharon let go of it.

—No, Sharon. Don't push! ——It's too early; don't —

She wiped Sharon's face.

—Don't push yet, Sharon.

Sharon gasped again.

—When!?

—In a little while. ——In ——Out ——

Sharon had to scream again, and gulp back air.

—It —it hurt more.

—Not much.

—Yes, much! Jeeesus!

* * *

They were all in the hall, watching Veronica, waiting. She was taking ages.

—Ah no, she said. ——Ah no; the poor thing.

She wouldn't look at them.

—Is she alright? ——Will you come home now? ——Get a taxi, Jimmy. You must be exhausted. ——That's terrible. ——Okay. In a while. Bye bye, love.

She put the phone down, and turned to them.

—A girl, she said.

—Yeow!

—Alive? said Darren.

He was crying.

—Yes!

—I thought —The way you were talkin' —

He started laughing.

The twins hugged Darren and Jimmy Jr and Veronica and Larrygogan. Les was out.

—What'll we call her? said Linda.

Veronica laughed.

—Hey, Larrygogan, said Tracy. —We've a new sister.

—She's not your sister, said Jimmy.

—Why?

—You're her auntie, he told her.

—Am I? Janey!

—So am I then, said Linda.

—That's righ', said Jimmy.

—I'm tellin' Nicola 'Malley, said Linda. —She thinks she's great just cos her ma lets her bring her sister to the shops. ——Come on, Tracy.

They were gone.

—Well, Darren, said Veronica. —Do you like being an uncle?

—Ah yeah, said Darren. —It's brilliant.

* * *

Sharon was able to look at her in the crib there without having to lift her head. That was nice.

There she was, asleep; red, blotched, shrivelled and gorgeous; all wrapped up. Tiny. And about as Spanish looking as —

She didn't care.

She was gorgeous. And hers.

She was fuckin' gorgeous.

Georgina; that was what she was going to call her.

They'd all call her Gina, but Sharon would call her George. And they'd have to call her George as well. She'd make them.

—Are yeh alrigh', love?

It was the woman in the bed beside Sharon.

—Yeah, said Sharon. —Thanks; I'm grand.

She lifted her hand —it weighed a ton —and wiped her eyes.

—Ah, said the woman. —Were yeh cryin'?

—No, said Sharon. —I was laughin'.

* * *

FOR THE BEST IN PAPERBACKS, LOOK FOR THE (penguin logo)

In every corner of the world, on every subject under the sun, Penguin represents quality and variety—the very best in publishing today.

For complete information about books available from Penguin—including Pelicans, Puffins, Peregrines, and Penguin Classics—and how to order them, write to us at the appropriate address below. Please note that for copyright reasons the selection of books varies from country to country.

In the United Kingdom: For a complete list of books available from Penguin in the U.K., please write to *Dept E.P., Penguin Books Ltd, Harmondsworth, Middlesex, UB7 0DA.*

In the United States: For a complete list of books available from Penguin in the U.S., please write to *Consumer Sales, Penguin USA, P.O. Box 999—Dept. 17109, Bergenfield, New Jersey 07621-0120.* Visa and MasterCard holders call 1-800-253-6476 to order all Penguin titles.

In Canada: For a complete list of books available from Penguin in Canada, please write to *Penguin Books Canada Ltd, 10 Alcorn Avenue, Suite 300, Toronto, Ontario, Canada M4V 3B2.*

In Australia: For a complete list of books available from Penguin in Australia, please write to the *Marketing Department, Penguin Books Ltd, P.O. Box 257, Ringwood, Victoria 3134.*

In New Zealand: For a complete list of books available from Penguin in New Zealand, please write to the *Marketing Department, Penguin Books (NZ) Ltd, Private Bag, Takapuna, Auckland 9.*

In India: For a complete list of books available from Penguin, please write to *Penguin Overseas Ltd, 706 Eros Apartments, 56 Nehru Place, New Delhi, 110019.*

In Holland: For a complete list of books available from Penguin in Holland, please write to *Penguin Books Nederland B.V., Postbus 195, NL-1380AD Weesp, Netherlands.*

In Germany: For a complete list of books available from Penguin, please write to *Penguin Books Ltd, Friedrichstrasse 10-12, D-6000 Frankfurt Main 1, Federal Republic of Germany.*

In Spain: For a complete list of books available from Penguin in Spain, please write to *Longman, Penguin España, Calle San Nicolas 15, E-28013 Madrid, Spain.*

In Japan: For a complete list of books available from Penguin in Japan, please write to *Longman Penguin Japan Co Ltd, Yamaguchi Building, 2-12-9 Kanda Jimbocho, Chiyoda-Ku, Tokyo 101, Japan.*